ESPECIALLY FOR GIRLS® Presents

Fantasy Summer

by SUSAN BETH PFEFFER

PACER BOOKS / New York

a member of The Putnam Publishing Group

This book is a presentation of **Especially for Girls**?
Weekly Reader Books. Weekly Reader Books offers
book clubs for children from preschool through
high school. For further information write to:
Weekly Reader Books, 4343 Equity Drive,
Columbus, Ohio 43228.

Edited for Weekly Reader Books and published by
arrangement with Pacer Books, a member of The
Putnam Publishing Group. Especially for Girls and
Weekly Reader are federally registered trademarks
of Field Publications.

Published by Pacer Books
a member of the Putnam Publishing Group
51 Madison Avenue
New York, New York 10010
Copyright © 1984 by Susan Beth Pfeffer
perfect image™ is a trademark
of The Putnam Publishing Group
Printed in the United States of America

Library of Congress Cataloging in Publication Data
Pfeffer, Susan Beth,
    Fantasy summer.   (Perfect Image)
Summary: Sixteen-year-old Robin's summer
in New York, as an intern on a teen
magazine, provides her with both happy
and sobering experiences that expand her
understanding of herself and other people.
[1. New York (N.Y.)—Fiction.   2. Friendship—
Fiction.   3. Self-perception—Fiction]   I. Title
PZ7.P44855Fan 1984   [Fic]   84-3236
ISBN 0-399-21086-5

1

WHY WOULDN'T THEY leave already?

Robin had been impatient for this day to come ever since the envelope arrived informing her that she'd been selected to be the photography intern at *Image, the* magazine for teenagers. Over seven thousand girls had applied, and Robin still couldn't believe she'd been one of the four girls who'd been picked. Now the biggest day in her life was finally here, and she wanted to meet the other girls without her parents around.

Robin Schyler genuinely loved her parents, and enjoyed spending time with them. She'd probably miss them the minute they left, but now she couldn't stop wishing they'd disappear on the spot.

"We can't possibly leave until we see Annie," Robin's mother said, as though she'd been reading Robin's mind. Robin reflected sadly that she probably had. One of those maternal gifts her mother claimed to have.

"This is a nice room," Robin's father said, checking out the closet. "Lots of storage space."

"It seems clean too," Robin's mother said. "I'll just check the bathroom to see if there are any cockroaches."

"Mom, you don't have to," Robin pleaded. "I can kill my own

cockroaches, honest." What if one of the other girls came in and found her mother on the bathroom floor?

"You'd better be able to," Robin's father said, advancing to the air conditioner. "New York in the summer is the roach capital of the world."

He played with some switches, and the soft whir of air conditioning began. "This is a good unit," he continued. "You can use it as white noise, to cover the street sounds."

"All right, Dad," Robin said. "If my roommate doesn't mind."

"She won't mind," Robin's mother said, emerging from the bathroom. "New York City nights practically demand air conditioning in the summer. It can get really brutal here."

Ever since Robin had heard from *Image* magazine, her mother had been giving her advice on life in New York City. Robin thought that her mother was actually more excited about the internship than she was.

Not that Robin hadn't been thrilled when the letter came telling her she'd been accepted. She thought of it more as winning, as though she'd bought just the right lottery ticket, and no amount of being told that she'd been selected because of her talent as a photographer really convinced her that it was anything more than luck that allowed her to be spending two months in New York working for the art director of *Image* magazine. *Image* was the magazine she'd aspired to subscribing to when she officially became a teenager. *Image* was the magazine her older sister, Caro, had read religiously and hoarded in her bedroom closet, where Robin wasn't allowed to search. *Image* was the one true sign you were a real American teenage girl, the sort you had always dreamed of being. The sort they showed on their pages, wearing fabulous clothes, doing marvelous things. Even the problems *Image* analyzed had a glamour to them. How to get the right boy to ask you out. Should you be a cheerleader? How to pick among all the colleges that were bound to desire your presence. There were no failures in *Image*. At worst, you needed a makeover, and if you couldn't go to the magazine to have it done for you, they'd show you just what to do to look like an *Image* model. As far as Robin was concerned, it was *the* magazine to read, and she suspected she was just one of millions of American teenage girls who felt exactly the same way.

Robin knew about the summer internships. You couldn't read *Image* and not know about them. Every year they had an issue practically devoted to them. Four girls picked from all over the United States to spend a summer working at *Image* and enjoying the exciting life of New York City. The girls all got made over, although in Robin's opinion she supposed they were always close to perfect even before the hair and makeup people started doing their magic. One intern even got to be on the cover of the magazine. Caro had thought of applying for an internship, but had decided instead to spend the summer between her junior and senior years working at the local newspaper as their summer teen editor. No one could have imagined she'd never have the chance again.

Knowing that Caro had considered applying made the idea of the summer internship a little more believable, but still Robin wouldn't have applied except that her mother practically forced her to. And that was because Annie's mother had called to say Annie was applying for the editorial internship.

Robin sighed, just thinking about Annie and her mother. It wasn't that Annie wasn't a perfectly okay cousin, and Aunt Gail was really okay one on one. But Aunt Gail was so competitive with Robin's mother, her twin sister. Maybe it had to do with their being fraternal twins. Maybe they were both just competitive people. Whatever the reason, Robin couldn't remember a time when Aunt Gail wasn't on the phone telling Robin's mother the extraordinary things Annie was accomplishing at that very moment. And naturally Robin's mother had to have stuff to throw back at Aunt Gail. So when Annie applied, it was only natural, at least to Robin's mother's way of thinking, that Robin apply too. The odds were that neither one of them would make it past the first cut, but why should Annie have the privilege of being the only one to be rejected?

When Robin's mother got into one of those moods, Robin had

learned long before just to give in and do what she asked for. Usually it wasn't too painful. Besides, she just might have entered on her own, although she doubted it. Robin wasn't that thrilled with the idea of rejection. She filled out the form they had printed in the magazine, and sent in a picture of herself, as well as two prints of photographs she'd taken that the magazine informed her she was never to expect to see again. Robin had the negatives, so that didn't disturb her.

A month later, much to her shock, Robin received a letter from *Image* asking her to fill out a much longer form, write a two-hundred-word essay about what she hoped to gain from a summer spent at *Image,* and shoot three photographs of different people, preferably not family members. Robin agonized over the long form, which asked her all kinds of questions she knew were nobody's business but her own, whipped off the two hundred words with hardly a thought, because she knew if she started thinking she'd never be able to write anything, and took pictures of the three best-looking girls in her high-school class. Who knows? she told them. Maybe *Image* would hire them as models.

Six weeks later, just when Robin had decided she had absolutely definitely not been selected, she got a letter from the editor-in-chief of *Image* welcoming her to the exciting world of *Image* magazine. There were more forms to fill out, releases for her parents to sign, information about the salary she'd be paid, the schedule for the summer, and a brochure about the Abigail Adams Hotel, where Robin would be staying under strict supervision all summer long.

Robin spent the rest of that afternoon going through the contents of the envelope over and over again. She checked at least three times to make sure they had her name and address down absolutely correctly. They sure seemed to, and to the best of her knowledge, there weren't any other Robin Louise Schylers in Elmsford, Ohio. At least not any other sixteen-year-old ones.

Whenever Robin looked up from the magic envelope, she saw her mother staring at the clock first, and then the telephone. Robin's father had been called at his office already, and Kevin, her younger brother, had been told the minute he came in from soccer practice, but there was still Aunt Gail to be informed. Robin was thoroughly ashamed of herself, but she couldn't help enjoying the image of Aunt Gail's face, hearing of Robin's triumph.

"I'll just give her five minutes," Robin's mother said when the clock finally reached five P.M. But before the five minutes were over, the phone rang.

"Why, hello, Gail," Robin could hear her mother saying. "I was just about to call you. What? But that's amazing. No, listen to me for a moment. Robin won too. Yes, isn't that something?"

Robin stopped listening. If she could have, she would have left the house immediately, but her mother called out to her to pick up the extension before she had the chance to escape. So she picked up the phone, and Annie did at her end, and the four of them were all on the phone at once marveling that out of seven thousand girls, two cousins had been picked for *Image* internships.

Robin hadn't see all that much of Annie in the past couple of years, but she could see the expression on her face just from looking at her own face in the mirror. Shock and horror were definitely the expressions for the day.

If there had been any way of convincing her parents that she no longer wanted the internship, Robin might have even tried. Who wanted to spend the summer with Annie? Who wanted to have her mother and her Aunt Gail on the phone constantly swapping their daughters' latest triumphs? It just wasn't worth it. But there was no way her parents would have fallen for it, and Robin's only hope was that Annie would drop out instead.

Which, of course, Annie didn't. Robin didn't blame her, but life would have been so much nicer if she had. Of course Annie was bound to feel the same way about her.

There was the sound of a key opening the lock to Robin's door. Robin and her parents looked toward the door to see who would be making an entrance. To Robin's undisguised horror, it was Annie.

"Oh," Annie said. She stood in the doorway flanked by two large suitcases. "Aunt Polly. Uncle Paul. Hi."

5

"Annie darling," Robin's mother said, and ran over to give her a big hug. Robin's father joined her, first in the hug and then to help carry Annie's bags into the room.

"I don't believe this," Robin's mother said. "You two girls will be roommates this summer. Wait until Gail hears. She'll be thrilled."

"Hi, Annie," Robin said.

"Robin," Annie said. "Did you have a good trip?"

"We certainly did," Robin's mother said. "And how was the train trip down?"

"Fine," Annie said. "Long."

"We're taking the shuttle flight up," Robin's father said. "Your parents said they'd pick us up at the airport."

"I know," Annie said. "They're really looking forward to a visit from you."

"It's just for the weekend," Robin's mother said. "But I'm looking forward to it too. I haven't been in Boston in years."

"This is a nice room," Annie said, looking around. "Boy, that air conditioner sure feels good."

"See, I told you your roommate wouldn't mind being cool in the summer," Robin's mother said, a little too triumphantly for Robin's taste. "It's a nice clean room too, Annie. Tell your mother I checked for cockroaches and didn't find a single one."

"They were all married roaches," Robin said, but only her father laughed. There were times when Robin just knew the only person who really understood her in the world was her father.

"It's been wonderful seeing you, Annie," Robin's father declared. "But Polly and I had better get going. We still have to go to the airport, and that isn't always easy from midtown Manhattan."

"Tell my parents I got here safely," Annie said.

"We certainly will," Robin's mother said.

Robin licked her lips nervously. "Don't forget what you promised, Mom," she said.

"What's that, honey?" her mother asked.

"About not calling," Robin said. "You said I could call you collect instead of your calling here all the time."

"Yes, dear," Robin's mother said with a sigh. "Did you give your mother such strict instructions, Annie? Or is she allowed to make contact with you every now and again?"

"Actually we arranged that I'd call home Sunday mornings," Annie said. "It seemed more convenient that way."

"That's a good idea," Robin's mother said. "All right, Robin, we'll expect a phone call from you every Sunday morning."

It was better than having them call her, Robin realized with a sigh. Besides, a quick agreement meant they'd leave before the other girls came and realized Robin's parents thought she was such a baby she couldn't be trusted to make it from Ohio to New York by herself. "Sure," she said. "That's a great idea, Mom. I'm sure I'll have plenty to tell you each week."

"Okay, that's settled," Robin's father said, glancing at his watch. "Come on, Polly. We really do have to get going."

Robin's mother hugged both girls and said good-bye. Robin's father hugged them too. Robin thought she caught a glimpse of tears in his eyes. She felt a little like crying herself at that point, although she wasn't sure just why.

The girls watched Robin's parents in the hallway until the elevator arrived, and then they closed the door. "Well," Annie said. "You really want to be roommates?"

"No," Robin said, a little too swiftly. "I mean, not unless you do."

"I think it's a lousy idea," Annie said. "As a matter of fact, I've been giving all this a lot of thought, and I think the fewer people who know we're cousins, the better."

"Nobody sounds good," Robin said. "It's nobody else's business anyway."

"Exactly," Annie said. "I know I don't want to be judged because of you. And I'm sure you don't want to be judged based on me either."

"Absolutely not," Robin said. "It can be our secret."

"It's too inhibiting otherwise," Annie said. "You want to stay in this room, or should I?"

"I'll swap," Robin said. "They said at the desk the other girls

7

are in Room 774, right next door. I'll go over there right now and see if they're in there already."

"I think they are," Annie said. "I think I heard the sound of girls talking there when I came in."

"I'll check," Robin said, happy for the excuse to leave the room. She walked the few feet to 774 and knocked.

"Coming," she heard a girl drawl, and in a few seconds someone opened the door. She was about Robin's height, Robin noticed automatically, but she probably weighed twenty pounds less. The girl was thinner than Robin ever dreamed of being. She had shoulder-length blond hair, hazel-green eyes, and was wearing a short purple dress that showed off endless miles of legs. Robin felt like a hick just looking at her.

"Hi," she managed to blurt out. "I'm Robin Schyler. One of the *Image* interns."

The girl smiled. "So are we," she said. "Is your roommate here yet? We've been dying of curiosity."

"She is," Robin said, and noticed that in the back of the room, standing by the window, was another girl. "Annie's here too, and this might sound a little weird, but we'd like to make a swap. Would one of you be willing to move in with Annie and let me use this room instead?"

"Why?" the first girl asked. "Is Annie a vampire or something?"

"I don't care," the second girl said. "I'll swap, Ashley. It'll be easier for me to move because I haven't unpacked yet."

"Thanks," Robin said. "I'll just go over to next door and get my stuff."

"Bring over Annie too," Ashley said. "We might as well all meet now and get it over with."

The other girl took two suitcases off one of the beds and followed Robin to the room next door.

"It's all okay," Robin told Annie. "They agreed to the switch."

"Great," Annie said, with the first sincere smile Robin had seen on her that day. "Hi, I'm Annie Powell."

"Torey Jones," the girl said. "Where should I put my bags?"

"This bed," Robin said, and walked over to it to take her own things off. "We're invited back next door," she told Annie. "See you there?"

"Sure," Annie said. "Need help with your bags?"

"That would be nice," Robin said, and Annie took one of the suitcases and followed Robin back to 774. Ashley was standing by the door waiting for them.

"Annie Powell," Annie said as she saw Ashley.

"Ashley Boone," Ashley said. "Come on in. Robin, I already took that bed, I hope you don't mind."

"Not at all," Robin said, plopping down on the other bed. Annie followed her with the second suitcase.

"I can't get over all of you," Ashley said. "You all brought so much. I hardly brought anything, so I'd have an excuse to buy all new clothes."

"My parents would kill me if I bought all new clothes," Annie said. "My mother and I have been shopping for weeks for this summer."

"I can't afford New York City clothes," Torey said.

"It just never occurred to me," Robin moaned. "I could have gotten a whole new New York wardrobe if I'd just thought of it."

"Stick with me, kid," Ashley said. "I'll teach you all kinds of things you never thought of before."

"Sounds like fun," Robin said, and almost to her surprise she meant it. A summer in New York, away from her family, almost away from Annie. A summer to herself, to grow up and learn. A summer to become a whole new person. She couldn't imagine anything better in the entire universe just then.

2

"WHO WANTS TO go first?" Annie asked as the girls settled awkwardly into silence. Robin decided to do something useful by unpacking her bags, but Annie, Ashley, and Torey were all sitting around looking like they should know what to be doing but didn't.

"I will," Ashley said. "My name is Ashley Boone and I'm from Ashley, Missouri. I live with my mother and her father, Mr. Ashley himself. I can't stand either one of them. My parents are divorced, and I don't care for my father either. My grandfather owns the town pretty much. It's the Ashley National Bank, and the Ashley *Gazette*, and KASH Radio. I'm not the only person in town to hate his guts, but I'm the one stuck with living with him. Someday he's going to die and then eventually my mother will too, and I'll inherit everything and sell it all and take the money and move as far away from Ashley, Missouri, as is humanly possible. That's all I live for, getting away from that dumb town. Next?"

"That's not fair," Annie said. "How do you expect anybody to beat that?"

"It's easy, believe me," Ashley replied. "How about if my

roomie goes next? Tell us all your dirtiest secrets, Robin."

Robin paused from putting her underwear away in the top drawer of the dresser to think about just what her dirtiest secret might be. "My name is Robin Schyler," she said, and then she giggled. "I think you've all heard that before," she explained. "I don't think I have any really dirty secrets. You know, except the normal ones. I cheated on an algebra test two years ago and didn't get caught, but I think about it sometimes. Does that count?"

"Not unless you cheat on a regular basis," Ashley declared.

"I don't," Robin said. "I'm really very wholesome and normal. I live with my parents and my younger brother in a small town in Ohio. It's a couple of hours away from Cleveland. My father's a doctor, and my mother works part-time as a librarian. I'm here to intern under the art director. I take photographs. I'm pretty good at that, actually. And that's just about it."

"We can't all be tormented," Ashley said cheerfully, "Besides, things will probably be a lot easier this summer if I'm the only one suffering all the time. At least in this room."

"Fine," Robin said. "I'll be the stable one. I can handle that."

"Me next, I guess," Annie said, and Robin went back to her unpacking. "My name is Anne Powell, but everybody calls me Annie. I live with my parents in Boston. Actually in the suburbs. And I have an older brother, but he's in college now. Michael. I mean, that's his name. My parents are both professors. There are a lot of professors in Boston. I am expected to do well in things, and I generally do. Only I'd like to do better. I really like being best at things. I'm going to be interning with the feature-articles editor. I've already been named as feature editor of my school newspaper for next year. I don't think I want to spend the rest of my life editing, though. It's just one of the few things a teenager can do that at least gives her the illusion of power. I think what I'd really like to do is be Secretary of State. Or maybe, if I could, the dictator of a small Latin-American country! I really think I was born to dictate."

Torey and Ashley laughed. Robin decided she was truly happy she and Annie agreed not be be judged on the other's behavior.

11

"We're down to you, Torey," Ashley said. "How do you feel, knowing you're rooming with a power freak for the entire summer?"

"Comforted somehow," Torey said.

Robin turned around to get a good look at Torey. She hadn't had that much of a chance to really check her out before. Once she looked, though, she was startled at what she'd missed.

First of all, Torey was tall, taller than any of the rest of them, and none of them was really short. Torey looked about five-feet-eight, or maybe even an inch or two taller. Her hair was genuinely blond, an assumption Robin was unwilling to make about Ashley's, even though Torey's hair color was considerably lighter. Her eyes were Paul Newman blue, and she had the kind of cheekbones models killed for. But it wasn't even that Torey was strikingly pretty. All the girls in the room were pretty, Robin realized. Even Annie, who, as always, was just a little plumper than she'd probably like. There was something more to Torey's looks. There was a maturity to her that Robin was unaccustomed to seeing in teenagers. Her face was almost powerful in its serenity and strength. Robin breathed a sigh of relief that she was rooming with Ashley instead of Torey. Wildly unhappy neurosis she could handle a lot more easily than all the self-assurance she could sense in Torey.

"I'm Victoria Jones," Torey began. "Torey for short. I have two younger sisters and a younger brother. We live with our parents in Raymund, New York, which is in the Catskills. The land we live on is very beautiful. We have a large garden, and grow just about all our own produce. We can what we don't eat in the summertime, and that helps us get through the winter. We keep chickens too, for their eggs."

"Do you live very far from New York?" Annie asked. "The Catskills are pretty close, aren't they?"

"It was a four-hour bus trip," Torey replied. "But the bus stopped everywhere. The summer people say it's a three-hour drive. This is my first time in New York, though, so I really don't know any better than that."

"You live three hours from New York and this is only your

12

first trip?" Ashley asked. "That's terrible. If I lived that close to New York, I'd be here constantly. I go to St. Louis constantly, that's how desperate I am."

"I guess I'm not desperate, then," Torey said. "It costs money to go to New York. You have to understand, we don't have any money for things like that."

"What do you have money for, then?" Ashley asked. Robin marveled at her nerve. Ashley was a girl with a dazzling lack of manners.

"Not a heck of a lot," Torey said, and smiled. "We get by, but it isn't easy. Nobody has a lot of money in Raymund except for the summer people."

"You mean you're poor," Ashley continued. "You're poor, and everybody in Raymund is poor, too. There aren't that many rich people in Ashley, either. My grandfather sees to that."

Torey laughed. Robin gave up unpacking and started watching. She didn't know either of the girls well enough to be sure, but it seemed to her they actually were enjoying each other. Annie, Robin noted, just looked uncomfortable.

"There are worse things than being poor in Raymund," Torey said. "It's a good town, and people really care there. When I found out I'd gotten the internship, my high school organized a car wash to get me the money for the bus ticket down. And the supermarket where I work had a flea market in its parking lot and the money went to buy me two new suitcases. The editor of the newspaper where I work part-time didn't give me anything, but he said when I got back I'd get a raise."

"How big is Raymund, anyway?" Annie asked.

"It's real small," Torey said. "I guess around three thousand in the summer, less in the winter. We all depend on the summer people and the hunters and fishermen."

"My family has a summer house," Ashley declared. "It's even worse than our winter house, because it's farther away from civilization. You're really stuck there. That's where I'd be now if this internship hadn't come through—at our summer house, spending July and August slowly going crazy."

13

"Don't do that here, okay?" Robin said. "I wouldn't mind, except we are roommates, and I can't stand the sight of crazy people."

"I'll keep that in mind," Ashley said. "Besides, this summer is going to be perfect. Didn't you know that? This is going to be the one perfect summer we'll all look back on when we get old and decrepit like my grandfather."

"I'd like this summer to be perfect," Robin admitted. "I could really use a perfect summer."

There was a knock at the door. Robin, still the only one standing, walked over and opened it.

"Oh, good, you're all here," a woman said, walking into the room. "My name is Jean Kingman and I'm publicity editor for *Image*. More to the point, I'm in charge of the four of you for this summer."

At that, all the girls examined her carefully. She looked to be in her early thirties, very attractive, and fashionably dressed. A genuine New York career woman, Robin decided. Just the kind they would all pretend to be this summer.

"First of all, call me Jean," the woman continued. "Different people are going to tell you to call them by their first names, or not, depending on who they are and how formal they are, but I'm a first-name sort of person. You have to be in publicity. I feel like I know you all already, but I guess I should say hello to you individually. You're Torey, right?" she said, advancing to the chair Torey was in.

Torey rose and shook Jean's hand. "I am," she said. "It's good to meet you."

"Likewise," Jean said. "And Robin opened the door for me, right?"

"Right," Robin said, uncertain whether she should go back to unpacking.

"Ashley," Jean continued. "That's a fabulous outfit, Ashley. Don't even think of wearing anything that short to the office. We are very conservative at *Image*."

"I'll be sure not to," Ashley said. "Thanks for the warning."

"And you're Annie," Jean said. "Oh, Annie, you've gained weight, haven't you?"

"A few pounds," Annie admitted. Robin turned around to give her cousin a closer examination. As far as she could see, Annie was her standard weight.

"That won't do at all," Jean said. "From now on you're on a strict diet. Ask Laura Cleary tomorrow for one. She's our health-and-nutrition editor, and believe me, she knows all the diets in the book. We can't have you so plump for your makeover session."

"All right," Annie said, and Robin could see she was blushing.

"The rest of you look fine," Jean said. "And Annie will too, after a month or so of dieting. You know one of you is going to be on the cover of the February issue of *Image*. That's really something to aspire to."

In spite of herself, Robin agreed. She wished it didn't matter to her, especially since she was sure she'd never be the one to be picked. But to be the cover girl of *Image*, if only once, was a dream so perfect it didn't matter that it was probably meaningless as well.

"You girls are going to have a wonderful summer," Jean assured them. "A summer girls all over America will be dreaming about. We expect you to work, of course. You're not here just to be paid tourists. But we have plenty of fun in store for you too."

Robin stopped unpacking. She wanted to learn as much about the work and the fun as she could.

"For starters, there's a small dinner party I'm here to herd you to tonight," Jean said. "Nothing fancy, and nothing too tiring, but we thought you might like to meet the editors you'll be working with and their assistants in a nonoffice situation. And we've arranged for you to go to the theater a few times each, and to a special press screening of the new Dan Keller movie. We're doing an interview with Dan, of course, to coincide with the opening of the movie. And since *Image* has corporate memberships to most of New York's museums, you'll have free admission to just about any museum you care to go to."

"Are we going to have any time to ourselves?" Ashley asked.

"Of course you are," Jean said. "I should have known you'd

15

be the one to ask that, Ashley. One girl does every summer. But we do have rules, fairly strict ones. They have to be strict, because we're in charge of you for the summer, and that's a heavy responsibility. The rules are going to sound pretty standard, but I have to tell you what they are. First of all, no drugs, no drinking, no nothing illegal. *Image* will not tolerate a scandal. And that is non-negotiable. Just one hint that you're drinking or taking drugs of any sort stronger than aspirin and you're out on your ear. Straight back to Mommy. Is that clearly understood?"

The girls nodded. It was a sensible rule, Robin knew, but she wished Jean hadn't sounded quite so stern about it.

"Now, about boys," Jean said. We have you staying in this convent of a hotel where no boys are allowed in your rooms. By the way, this also greatly increases the safety of this hotel, which is the other major reason you're staying here. New York is not always a safe place to be, especially if you're not used to it. But that's a whole other topic. As a matter of fact, at lunch on Monday one of the other editors is instructed to give you a safety lecture. I'm here to tell you about the rules and regulations."

"Are there more?" Ashley asked. Robin was grateful to her for being willing to ask the attention-getting, absolutely necessary questions.

"We were discussing boys," Jean said. "*Image* wants you to have a great summer, and that obviously involves boys. There's going to be a large party for you next weekend, and another one at the end of the summer, and if any of you need an escort for those parties, we will happily supply you with one. If you meet a nice boy during the course of the summer, of course you can go out with him and have a fine time. We will not be chaperoning you twenty-four hours a day, any more than your parents would be. But there are curfews that you'll be expected to obey. Eleven o'clock on weekdays, and midnight on weekends. You'll sign in every evening downstairs in the lobby, and if you haven't by one minute past curfew, someone at *Image*, probably me, will be immediately notified. We'll allow two curfew violations during the summer, if they aren't outrageous. You know, ten minutes or so

16

late, we'll forgive you twice. Three strikes and you're out. And if you're a half-hour late the first time, you'll be on probation for the rest of the summer, and believe me, that won't be a lot of fun for any of us. Any questions?"

Ashley was silent. So Robin was surprised when Annie was the one to open her mouth.

"My grandmother lives out on Long Island," she said. "And she wants me to visit her for a weekend soon. Actually she said all the girls were invited. How do I handle that?"

"You go and you have a great time," Jean said. "Just have your grandmother call me so we can arrange the details. Honestly, girls, *Image* wants you to be happy this summer, and that certainly includes visits with grandmothers. You can check out of the hotel for a weekend, if you're going to stay with anybody your parents have approved of before you got here. That was one of those endless forms your parents filled out for us, a list of people you could visit. But believe me, all those weekend visits will be carefully checked out. Don't think you can say you're visiting Granny and go off to the Hamptons for the weekend with some fabulous Columbia student you just met. You won't get away with it. Is that clearly understood?"

"Are the big parties fancy?" Torey asked. "I didn't bring anything fancy to wear."

"Not too fancy," Jean said, smiling warmly at her. "I'm sure if we have to, we can improvise something. Ashley can help. She's our fashion apprentice, after all."

Robin made a quick mental inventory of the clothes she'd brought, and said a silent thank-you to her mother, who had insisted she bring two party dresses.

"One final note, and then I'll be going," Jean said. "I have a couple of errands to run, and then I'll meet you downstairs in the lobby to take you to the party in an hour. That should be enough time for you all to shower and change."

Robin waited nervously to learn the last, and presumably worst, restriction on them.

"New York can be a big, scary, tough city," Jean said. "And

17

just being away from your parents can be an unsettling situation. I want you to know I'm here to help you. If you have any questions or any problems, feel free to ask me. I'm going to be handing each of you some papers. On one of them is the basic schedule for this summer. We have some events already prescheduled, like next week's radio appearance and the TV interview we have set up for next month. National cable, so that should be a special incentive to you, Annie, to lose those pounds."

Annie scowled. Robin didn't blame her.

"I also have listed local churches and synagogues if any of you would like to attend services," Jean continued.

"Oh, good," Torey said.

"And at the top of every piece of paper I've listed both my office and home phone numbers," Jean said. "I have a machine, so if I'm not in, you can leave a message for me, and I'll get back to you as soon as possible. The editors you'll be specifically working with are also likely to give you their home numbers, so you'll have some backups if you need them. Don't hesitate to call if you need help. We want to make everything as easy and pleasant for you as we possibly can. Is that understood?"

The girls all murmured yes.

"Fine," Jean said, getting up. "Now I'll be leaving, to give you all a chance to curse me out in private. I'll meet you in one hour, and I don't like to be kept waiting. Nobody at *Image* does. Keep that in mind when you start work tomorrow. All right. See you downstairs in an hour." She walked to the door and let herself out.

"She took her chains and shackles with her," Ashley said. "You think we should call her back and remind her?"

"She had some nerve harping on Annie's weight like that," Robin said. "Like it was some kind of crime not to be skinny."

"When you're at somebody else's party, you have to play by their rules," Torey declared. "They want us to be as free from problems as possible. And that includes having us weigh what's right for their cameras."

"Torey's right," Annie said with a sigh. "I just don't know how

I'm going to manage a dinner party when I'm absolutely famished and I can't eat anything."

"How am I going to manage all of New York City when I'm psychologically famished and can't eat a thing either?" Ashley asked. "Just how much wild living do they think I can cram in before eleven o'clock at night?"

"More than most of us could even dream of," Torey said. "Come on, Annie. Let's get back to our room and become perfect for tonight."

"I will if you will," Annie said, and followed Torey out of the room.

Robin watched them leave, and then looked at Ashley. A summer spent with a saint, a sinner, and a would-be dictator on a diet. Just the sort of summer the readers of *Image* were dreaming about at that very moment. In spite of herself, she smiled. That would certainly be the last time she believed what she read in the magazines.

3

IT WAS MORE confusing than the first day at a new school.

Meeting some of the editors at a small dinner the night before had probably been a great idea, Robin reflected as she tried to keep track of everything her guide, Shelley Haslitt, was showing her. But she'd come close to falling asleep in her salad bowl, and by the time the main course was served, her mind had stopped functioning altogether. She just hoped nobody judged her based on her behavior that night. She couldn't even remember speaking, just nodding when she thought that was appropriate.

Someone—the editor-in-chief, she thought—had said something about how the girls were probably exhausted, so presumably they were all excused. The funny thing was that Ashley, who had come the longest distance, was the most sparkling of them all. Annie had mostly been quiet, staring hungrily at the food, which she wasn't allowing herself to eat. And Torey had showed a cool reserve, which Robin envied. Torey could have been sleepwalking, for all she knew, but it just appeared that she was graciously making a royal appearance. Robin had merely felt middle-class and sleepy.

"Ladies' room over there," Shelly continued as she led Robin through the maze of corridors and offices that constituted the home of *Image* magazine. "There's the sample kitchen. They're forever trying out new recipes there, wonderful high-caloric things. You have to be real careful when you walk around here, because one of them will just grab you and demand you try something out for them. I gained ten pounds my first year here just from that kitchen. It was brutal trying to take them off."

Robin hoped Annie's office was nowhere near the kitchen.

"I was an intern one summer," Shelley declared as she allowed Robin quick peeks into conference rooms and editors' offices. "Twelve years ago. It was a great summer."

"Was that how you got this job?" Robin asked, hoping she remembered from the night before just what Shelley's job was. Assistant art director, she thought, but she'd met so many people the night before, it was hard to be sure.

"It was certainly a help," Shelley replied. "Hi, Donna," she called to the woman who was showing Ashley around. Ashley looked like she belonged right there. She was even dressed similarly to Donna, whoever she was. Robin felt very schoolgirlish in her skirt and blouse. Not that Ashley wasn't wearing a skirt and blouse herself. Just a different, more sophisticated sort of skirt and blouse. Robin resolved to buy a whole new wardrobe, even if she had to sell her old one to be able to afford it.

"There's so much to remember," Robin said, figuring she wasn't going to fool anyone by pretending to understand any of what was going on.

"My first week here, I was in a total fuddle," Shelley confided. "I remember feeling like a fool, and I was sure everybody knew what an idiot I really was, and they were bound to send me back to Tacoma, Washington, at any moment. My second week here, I just knew they were keeping me here for the sake of charity."

"But then it got better?" Robin asked, trying to keep the hope out of her voice.

"It sure did," Shelley said. "That's Mrs. Brundege's office. She was editor-in-chief here when I interned that summer, but she'd just started, so she was a little less intimidating. Not a lot, but a little. We called her Mrs. Brundege then, and we call her Mrs. Brundege now. I suggest you do so also."

It had never occurred to Robin to call Mrs. Brundege by her first name. She was startled to learn Mrs. Brundege even had a first name. The woman reminded Robin strongly of her elementary-school principal, a woman Robin had spent years in mortal terror of. Only Mrs. Brundege had a wardrobe that probably cost the equivalent of her principal's yearly salary. Everyone at *Image* dressed wonderfully except for herself. And Torey. Even Annie looked just right.

"She's really a nice person," Shelly said. "And not at all stuffy. But she's in charge, and she knows it, and you'd better know it as well. Which is perfectly reasonable, I suppose. This is the studio."

The studio. Finally. Robin hoped Shelley would let them linger here for a while, but she was too nervous to ask.

"Is it like what you imagined?" Shelley asked as she and Robin walked in. "I know it didn't match my image at all when I first saw it."

It didn't look like what Robin had imagined either. She'd pictured something large and white and airy, with a couple of huge lights, one incredibly handsome photographer snapping endless pictures of glamorous models who were swirling around to the sounds of the latest hit rock album. Instead there was a massive number of lights, none of which were on, endless wires on the floor, which Robin knew she was going to trip over, and open shelves loaded with all kinds of gadgets and clamps and tools. Everything seemed dark gray, and instead of a beautiful model, there was a small table set up with a plate, a napkin, and an empty glass.

"I know," Shelley said. "It really is a disappointment, isn't it? *Image* has a staff photographer, he's around somewhere, and he has an assistant, and we even have a darkroom to develop the black-and-white prints, but we only use it for still lifes and food shots. We hire outside for fashion and glamour. Most magazines use outside photographers for everything, but Mrs. Brundege likes to have someone on staff, and Herb is a great food photographer. Well, you know how great the food looks in *Image* every month."

Robin nodded. If all they shot at the magazine was food, did that mean she wasn't going to do any of the exciting photography she'd dreamed of doing all spring? If all they wanted her for was to take pictures of cookies and hot dogs, then why did they ask for photographs of people?

"There's a food-shooting session planned for this morning," Shelley said. "If you want, you can certainly watch as it's done."

"I'd like that," Robin said. It might come in handy someday to be able to take pictures of sandwiches. And anything she could learn about professional photography was better than nothing.

"I wanted to weep when I first saw that studio," Shelley said. "I think that was even a worse disappointment than when I found out I wasn't picked as the cover girl. Of course the girl my summer who did get picked for the cover went on to a very successful career as a model, so the competition wasn't really fair. We all knew she'd be picked, because she was just so gorgeous, but I couldn't help fantasizing that they'd pick me just because I was so much more average-looking. That's a basic lesson for you to learn about *Image*. Their idea of average is our idea of perfect. The sooner you learn that, the faster you move ahead here."

"Jean told Annie, one of the other interns, that she had to lose weight immediately," Robin said. "Annie isn't skinny, but she's pretty normal-looking. Probably most of *Image*'s readers look just like her."

"But they don't want to see pictures of girls who look like themselves," Shelley said. "They want dream images of themselves instead. Perfect skin, perfect figures, perfect clothes. *Image* peddles fantasy, the same as all the other fashion magazines. Only *Image* specializes in teenage fantasy."

"Is that good?" Robin asked.

Shelley shrugged her shoulders. "When I interned here, years ago, I didn't think it was," she said. "In the early seventies, we were all determined to see the truth come out about everything. But now I'm not so sure. If you can't have fantasies about life when you're a teenager, when can you? Besides, I'm absolutely addicted to decorating magazines, and I'll never have a home that looks like anything I've ever seen in *House and Garden*. Not at New York City rents, anyway."

Robin looked at Shelley carefully. She looked a lot like Jean had the night before, wearing just a little bit of makeup, but with a great, obviously well-tended hairstyle. Robin brushed her own back from her forehead self-consciously. Jean and Shelley also had slender, well-exercised bodies. But mostly what they had was a look of total self-confidence. Torey had had it when she'd stood up the night before to shake Jean's hand. Robin would never have it, unless they figured out a way to sell it in specialty shops at her local mall. She sighed with thoughts of her own inadequacy.

"Cheer up," Shelley said. "See, here we are back at the art director's offices." They walked into the small suite of rooms they'd started out from. "Alice, are you in?"

"I certainly am," Alice Abrams said, coming into the outer office. "Did you enjoy your tour, Robin?"

"I think I'm dizzy," Robin admitted. "There was so much to take in."

"Nobody expects you to master it all at once," Alice said with a cheerful smile. She was in her early forties and reminded Robin of her second-year French teacher, only without the accent. Except Alice Abrams was the art director of *Image*, which made her Robin's boss, and Shelley's boss, and the boss of lots of other people as well. So Robin knew not to feel too comfortable with her just because she reminded her of home.

"I think I showed Robin all the significant things," Shelley said. "Except, of course, where we keep our supply of incredibly good-looking male models."

"Well, that we don't show just anybody," Alice said. "You have to be here for at least two weeks before we show you that closet."

Robin laughed. She prayed it didn't come out as a giggle.

"I told Robin about the shoot set for this morning," Shelley said. "She seemed to be interested in seeing it. Right, Robin?"

"Definitely," Robin said, trying to sound definite.

"Fine," Alice said. "Herb can be a real bear, so don't pay any attention to him if he growls at you. Unless he tells you to do something, like get out of his way. Herb is the boss in that studio—not that he'll let you forget it."

"Herb was here when I interned that summer," Shelley said. "He was grumpy then too."

"Can I ask a question before I go there?" Robin asked.

"Of course," Alice replied. "Ask away."

"What am I going to be doing here this summer?" Robin asked. "I mean, what exactly is my job?"

Alice and Shelley laughed. Robin didn't know what kind of a sign that was, and didn't join in.

"You'll be doing lots of things," Alice said. "Very little of it glamorous. At least not here, with me. Basically you're spending the summer at *Image* for two reasons. First of all, and most important, you're here to learn about magazines, how they're put together, how they work. In order to do that, we'll mostly have you work as a gofer. You'll run errands, chase people down, and generally keep out of the way and behave yourself. And if you prove to be reliable, we'll give you some more interesting jobs. For example, if we think you can be trusted with it, we'll send you to take some black-and-white pictures of Jennifer Fitzhugh when we interview her."

That one took Robin by surprise. Jennifer Fitzhugh was one of the hottest young actresses on TV. In none of her springtime fantasies had Robin imagined herself actually taking pictures of somebody that famous for *Image*.

"That's part of the *Image* internship tradition," Shelley said. "We send the writing intern to do the interview and the art intern to take pictures of the two of them. It'll be in the same issues as your makeovers."

Robin nodded, trying to act as though her heart was beating at its usual steady pace. Actually this was the moment she'd dreamed of, the moment when she finally realized she was at *Image* for the summer, that it was all real. She'd be taking pictures of Jennifer Fitzhugh. She'd be made over. She might even be on the cover. The dream was real.

"The other reason why you girls are at *Image* is the fun reason," Alice said. "We want you to have the sort of summer our readers want you to have. In other words, perfect. Full of parties and fun events and good old-fashioned glamour. Carriage rides in Central Park. Boat tours around Manhattan. Sightseeing. Shopping. TV interviews. Makeovers. Modeling. Handsome young men. Just the slightest touch of romance. Perfection."

It certainly sounded that way to Robin.

"The trade-off is an almost total lack of privacy," Alice continued. "And not a heck of a lot of freedom. You might be enjoying running around here one day, doing errands for me or Shelley, when suddenly someone will summon you for an interview with some high-school-newspaper editor or a luncheon with some of the other editors."

"More to the point, you might have one of those fabulous over-by-eleven dates with a handsome young man and then have to cancel it at the last minute because someone at *Image* has arranged something altogether different for you that night," Shelley said. "That happened to me at least three times my summer here, and it cost me two boyfriends. Of course boys should be more tolerant now of the demands a career makes on a girl."

"Don't count on it," Alice said. "Basically for the next eight weeks you belong to *Image*, body and soul. Some girls can't take that."

"When you're at someone else's party, you have to play by their rules," Robin quoted sagely.

"Exactly," Alice said. "You catch on fast."

Robin had the feeling it was Torey who caught on fast, but she was willing to take the credit.

"End of lecture," Alice said. "Poor Robin. You've been in New York for twenty-four hours and your head must be spinning. We'll treat you easy today, don't worry."

"I can handle it," Robin said. For all she knew, she could, too.

"Fine," Alice said. "Then I'll give you your first job. I want you to take these sketches to Herb. He'll need them for the shoot. Do you think you can find your way back to the studio?"

"If I'm allowed to ask people directions," Robin replied.

"You certainly are," Alice said. "That's a good basic rule. If you don't know, ask. These are sketches of the way I want the photographs to look. Want to see?"

"I'd love to," Robin said. Alice spread out the pictures on Shelley's desk. Sure enough, there were four penciled sketches of food on dishes. "Cupcakes?" Robin asked.

"Cupcakes," Alice said. "January is always such a tough issue to put out. Nothing interesting to focus on between Christmas and Valentine's Day. So we're doing a lot of sports stuff this year. These are cupcakes with little footballs and basketballs iced on them."

"Wholesome cupcakes," Shelley added. "Made with carrots and zucchini."

"Zucchini cupcakes," Alice said with a shudder. "Food isn't my department. Making the food look good is my job, that's all. Take the sketches in to Herb and tell him I'll be there in a half-hour or so to see how things are going."

"All right," Robin said, and held the sketches as though they were a first-folio Shakespeare. She found her way to the studio more easily than she'd anticipated, and that made her feel better about things immediately.

The studio was busy. There were lights on, and a young man was setting them up so they lighted the table. There was food on the plates now too, being fussed over by a woman Robin didn't remember seeing before. The man who just had to be Herb was also in the studio, checking things out through the large camera set up on a tripod facing the table.

"Herb?" Robin asked, approaching him carefully.

"Yeah, what?" he asked, not bothering to look at her.

"I brought the sketches from Alice," Robin said, trying to sound assured.

"Oh, good," Herb said. "It's about time." He walked away from the camera and took the sketches from Robin's hand. Robin found she was reluctant to give them up. Maybe now that Herb had them, he'd kick her out of the studio. "Yeah, they're pretty much what I expected. Thanks, kid."

"You're welcome," Robin said, backing away carefully.

"You the new intern?" Herb asked, still looking down at the sketches.

"Yes, sir," Robin said.

"Wanna stay here and watch?" he asked. "You gotta swear to stay out of the way, though."

"I'd love to," Robin said. "I swear."

"I swear too," Herb said with a grin. "We'll have to have a cussing contest someday."

Robin laughed. Herb laughed harder.

"Okay, stand back in a corner and keep your mouth shut," Herb instructed her. "Maybe you'll learn a thing or two this summer."

"I sure hope so," Robin replied. "Oh, Alice said she'd be here in about half an hour."

"Good," Herb said. "Thanks, kid."

"You're welcome," Robin said, and walked over to what she hoped was a safely neutral spot.

The woman who'd been fussing with the food paused for a moment and joined Robin. "I'm Marlene Isaacs," she said. "Food stylist. You're Robin, right?"

"Right," Robin said. "The food looks great."

"Well, that's just the stand-in food," Marlene said. "They're in the kitchen now finishing up the real stuff for the photographs."

"I wouldn't mind a taste of the stand-in when Herb's through with it," Robin said. "Do all of you get to sample it when you're done?"

"Never touch the food," Marlene said. "Not the stuff that's used for photographs. Never. It's full of chemicals and stuff to make it look good under the lights. It's poison, Robin. We have to throw it away really carefully so bums don't dig it out from the garbage cans and eat it."

"You're kidding," Robin said. "You mean none of that food is edible?"

"Not that gets photographed," Marlene replied. "Is that understood?"

"Absolutely," Robin said, inching away slightly from the table where the food was being lighted. So the food was all poison. She wondered how millions of *Image*'s readers would feel about that one if they ever found out.

But then Robin smiled. The one reader she'd be sure to tell was Annie. Maybe that was just the diet trick she needed to become the symbol of perfection all of them—and all that food—were supposed to be.

4

ROBIN WAS LYING on her bed Thursday afternoon, hoping that she would never have to put on a pair of shoes again, when Ashley barged into the room. Nobody had warned her that having a summer internship would be so hard on the feet. Most of her job was running around, just as Alice had promised. Thus far Robin had run around to everybody's satisfaction, but it was proving rougher on her feet than she ever would have dreamed. She made a solemn vow never to get a job as a waitress.

"Are you napping?" Ashley asked Robin, while plopping down on Robin's bed. That way, if Robin had been asleep, she'd be bound to wake up. Robin had known Ashley for less than a week, but she was starting to figure out a lot of her tricks.

"Wide-awake," Robin admitted. "Just resting my feet forever."

"You're sixteen years old," Ashley said. "You're in the most exciting city in the world, and you finally have some time to yourself, and what do you do with it? You rest your feet. Is this how our *Image* readers imagine you?"

"They can imagine me any way they want," Robin said. "My feet hurt. Don't your feet hurt?"

"What's pain?" Ashley said. "Come on, rise and shine. We have a city to conquer."

"Ashley . . ." Robin grumbled, but she did sit up. Ashley smiled at the approaching triumph.

Robin wasn't sure why she allowed Ashley to bully her into things, but she did, and just then she was too tired to puzzle out the answer. The funny thing was, she liked Ashley enormously. If any of her friends at home had been so bossy, she would have killed them, but with Ashley it just amused her. And Ashley was right; it was foolish to waste a beautiful July afternoon hiding in a hotel room with swollen feet.

"I thought shopping," Ashley informed her. "And then dinner and a movie. We can do all that and be back here by eleven easy."

"Earlier than eleven, please," Robin said. "I never seem to get enough sleep. I absolutely swore to myself I'd go to bed early tonight."

"Ten, then," Ashley said. "We can go to an eight-o'clock showing of a movie and be back here by ten-fifteen at the absolute latest. How does that sound?"

Robin admitted sadly to herself that it did sound better than staying in the hotel room and watching reruns on TV. "All right," she said. "But the minute it turns into a late night, I'm coming straight back."

"It won't, I promise," Ashley said. "Put on some sneakers for your feet, and let's go see if Torey and Annie want to join us."

"Okay," Robin said. Sneakers sounded wonderful. If Ashley had even mentioned the word "shoes" it would have been hotel rooms and reruns for the night.

Ashley watched Robin get ready with glittering impatience. Robin deliberately took a few moments extra just for the pleasure of seeing Ashley struggle to stand still. Finally Robin had to admit she was ready, and the two girls went next door and knocked.

Torey opened the door. "Hi," she said. "What's up?"

"Adventure," Ashley said. "Can we come in?"

"Sure," Torey said, and Robin and Ashley soon found places to perch.

"Shopping," Ashley said. "Dinner in a real New York City restaurant. And then a movie. Maybe even something with subtitles. How does that sound?"

"Expensive," Torey said.

"Exhausting," Annie said. She was lying on her bed in a position Robin recognized as being identical to the one she herself had been in just a few short minutes before.

"Don't worry about expensive," Ashley said to Torrey. "I'll treat you."

"That isn't necessary," Torey said. "I don't have to go."

"But I want you to," Ashley said. "Dinner won't be that expensive, and neither will the movie. I can afford to pay for you. Besides, you've got to have some fun while you're here. You can't just work and save up your money."

"I'm not saving up my money," Torey said. "I'm sending it home to my family. And I am having fun. I'm having lots of fun. You don't have to worry about me, Ashley."

"I'm not worrying," Ashley replied. "I figure it's just an investment. You're the only one out of the four of us who is bound to be wildly successful. I'm going to go through my inheritance in no time flat once I finally inherit it. This way you'll remember me as that nice person who helped you out when you were down on your luck, and you'll treat me to all kinds of goodies in my old age. If I ever make it to old age. I'd like to put in right now for lots of beautiful young men. Want to make a note of that?"

Torey laughed. "What if I'm not successful?" she asked.

"I'll take my chances," Ashley said. "Besides, that way it can go down as one of my rare good deeds. I have no intention of becoming a philanthropist with the old man's millions."

"Have a good time, girls," Annie said, still not moving from her bed. "Send me a postcard."

"I have never seen such a collection of lazybones," Ashley said. "What's your excuse, Annie?"

"I don't have an excuse," Annie said. "I'm just not in the mood to wander around while you shop."

"You can shop too," Ashley said.

"I don't need anything," Annie said. "And I'd love to have some time absolutely alone without anybody around. Understand?"

"I think she's trying to tell you something, Torey," Ashley said. "Okay, Annie. Have your quiet time. But think of us exploring New York while you moan and whimper by yourself tonight."

"I'll certainly try to remember," Annie replied. " 'Bye girls. Have a good time. Stay out as late as you like."

"I only wish," Ashley grumbled.

Torey brushed her hair, grabbed her bag, and the girls were off.

"Mass transit," Torey declared.

"Certainly," Ashley said. "I thought we might try Greenwich Village. We can take the Fifth Avenue bus down. And then when we go back uptown tonight, we can take a cab."

"I can't afford a cab," Torey said.

"You'll give us the cost of the bus," Ashley said. "Robin and I can split the rest. Okay, Robin?"

"Fine," Robin said. "Just as long as dinner isn't at some really expensive place."

"I thought we'd eat ethnic and cheap," Ashley said. "I want to eat all the sorts of food you don't get to have in Ashley, Missouri."

"Something exotic," Torey said.

"Some country we've never even heard of," Ashley said. "Come on, girls, I see a bus coming."

In spite of her feet, Robin managed to run the few yards to the bus stop. Sure enough, just after they arrived, the bus did also. Robin dropped some coins into the change collector and pushed and shoved along with Ashley and Torey to find a place to stand. It was still rush hour, and there were no seats to be had.

The crowd thinned out as the bus drove straight down Fifth Avenue. Robin didn't bother getting a seat, since she wasn't sure whether she'd ever bother to stand up again if she sat down, but she was better able to see out the windows. They weren't on the glamorous part of Fifth Avenue, but it was still Fifth Avenue in New York City.

"Last stop," the bus driver announced as they reached Fifth Avenue and Eighth Street. Robin could see the arch at Washington Square Park. She regretted having worn sneakers. Probably nobody in all of Washington Square Park was wearing sneakers.

The girls got off the bus and looked around. On one side were beautiful brownstones. Robin could just imagine what the homes were like inside. Beautiful people, all novelists and painters, in apartments with brick walls and lots of bookshelves and fireplaces. They were probably all preparing at that very moment for dinner parties with other beautiful novelists and painters. They probably wouldn't even recognize a sneaker, let alone wear one.

On the other side was Washington Square Park, which was loaded with people. There were people running, and people playing Frisbee, and people playing with kids, and people playing with dogs, and people just playing guitars. It wasn't a big park, but it certainly was a busy one. Robin could spot an occasional bum and some bag ladies to boot, but it still looked like the friendliest park in the world. Robin yearned to be part of that carefree world.

"This is so great," Ashley said for all of them. "This is what I've dreamed of for so long."

"Come on," Torey said after a moment. "We have to do something. We can't let down the millions of readers of *Image* magazine."

"Shopping," Ashley proclaimed. "Let's find a fabulous Village boutique where I can spend scads of money on clothes they won't let me wear to work."

The girls walked down Eighth Street, which certainly didn't lack for stores. None of them were what Ashley wanted, though. It took a few blocks of walking on side streets before the boutique of Ashley's dreams materialized.

"This is it," she declared, practically pushing the other girls in.

"Boy, does this look expensive," Robin said. Torey didn't say anything, but Robin could see how wide her eyes had gotten.

Ashley didn't seem to care what the prices were on the clothes. She went through rack after rack with abandon, taking things out, analyzing them, and then putting them back. To entertain herself while Ashley shopped, Robin started looking around too. She found a blouse she loved. It was short-sleeved, eggshell-colored silk. Very grown-up, Robin felt. Not dissimilar to blouses she'd seen Alice and Shelley wear.

"That's a beautiful blouse," Ashley told her. "Very classic."

"It also costs a fortune," Robin said. "Just about all my spending money for the week."

"But it's an investment," Ashley said. "You could wear that when you go for college interviews. Try it on."

Robin took the blouse to the try-on room and put it on. Silk, she found, felt like nothing else in the world. It was like wearing warm butter. With a sigh she realized she never wanted to take the blouse off.

"Let us see," Ashley commanded, so Robin came out with the blouse on.

"Oh, Robin, it looks great," Torey said. "That's a wonderful color for you."

"It is very becoming," the saleswoman said.

"A real investment," Ashley said. "A blouse you can wear forever."

Robin stared at herself in the mirror. The blouse looked wonderful on her, even though she was wearing jeans and sneakers with it. With the right skirt, it would probably be the most perfect blouse in creation. And it did look startlingly good on her. It made her look older, but not artificially so. Just more self-assured, like Torey and Ashley. More in control of things. More grown-up.

Besides, her first week in New York was practically over with and she had hardly spent any money at all. All her meals had been taken care of up until then, and this was her first trip without an *Image* editor guiding her about and paying for transportation. She'd bought a bunch of postcards to send to people, but she didn't even have to buy stamps; her mother had made her pack a batch of them when she left Ohio. In the whole week, she'd just bought postcards, and some ice cream, and a couple of magazines, and that had been it. And her plans for the rest of the week were real inexpensive too. She was going out for the weekend to visit Annie's grandmother. That would just be train fare. So why not?

"I'll take it," Robin whispered.

"Good for you," Ashley said. "You're never going to regret it, Robin. It's such a perfect blouse."

"It is, isn't it?" Robin said, having doubts already. She went back to the try-on room and took the blouse off. When she put her T-shirt on, she found she missed the feel of the silk on her body. Someday she'd be so rich her entire wardrobe would be made of silk, T-shirts, jeans, and sneakers.

In all, the girls went into four stores. After the first one, Robin didn't even glance at the temptations. Instead she watched Ashley try things on. Torey looked things over casually, but Ashley really checked things out. After four shops, though, Robin was the only one to have spent any money.

"That's not fair," she complained as the girls started hunting around for an exotic restaurant. "How come you were the one who insisted on shopping, and I'm the one who ended up bankrupt?"

"It's important for me to see how things look," Ashley said. "I am in fashion, after all."

"You mean this was just research for you?" Robin asked.

"Not entirely," Ashley said. "If I had found something as perfect as your blouse, I would have bought it."

"It is a perfect blouse, isn't it?" Robin said, wishing she could remember a little better what it looked like.

"Silk is so wonderful," Ashley said. "It's like roses and champagne."

"And food," Torey said. "I'm famished. How does this place look?"

"Thai cuisine," Robin read out loud. "Well, somebody gave it two stars."

"Thai food is not big in Ashley, Missouri," Ashley declared. "So it's fine by me."

"Let's try it," Torey said. "Worse comes to worst, we'll cancel our trip to Thailand."

The girls walked into the restaurant. It wasn't very busy, and they were soon shown to a comfortable booth. Robin rested the bag with her blouse carefully by her side. She could wear it all summer long, she told herself, if she could find some skirts perfect enough to go with it.

The waiter brought them their menus and glasses of ice water, which they all gratefully gulped down. The menus took longer to digest, since none of the food was familiar to them.

They finally settled on fish, beef, and chicken dinners. That way they could each try what the others had ordered. The waiter took their order, refilled their water glasses, and walked away.

"I love New York," Robin said dreamily. "And think, after this, a movie."

"It isn't just New York," Ashley said. "It's the independence. It's the freedom of being away from parents and grandparents and editors. Have you noticed how everybody's treated us like adults?"

"I love it all," Robin said. "I especially love my blouse."

"I can't wait to be a grown-up," Ashley said. "It doesn't seem fair somehow that you have to go through so many preliminaries before you officially grow up. I'm ready for R-rated movies. I'm probably ready for X-rated ones, if you want to know the truth. Why should I have to wait?"

"You don't have to be so impatient," Torey replied. "Enjoy the time you're stuck being young. There's all the time in the world waiting for us. That's the one thing everybody has. Time."

"That's just not true," Robin said. "Not everybody has time."

The other girls turned to face her.

"Sometimes you think you have forever, but you don't," Robin said, feeling her face turn red. "My sister, Caro, she thought she had all the future, but then she was in an accident and she didn't have any time left at all."

"I didn't know you had a sister," Torey said. "You just mentioned a brother."

"Caro was older than me," Robin said. "She died from the injuries two years ago. She was seventeen."

"Oh," Ashley said. "I'm sorry, Robin."

"It must still hurt," Torey said.

37

"It'll hurt forever," Robin said. "But it taught me one thing, and that is not to assume you can do something tomorrow. You might not have a tomorrow. Not everybody gets to have a tomorrow."

"Well, I'd better get more than my share of time," Ashley said. "Because my yesterdays have been just terrible, and my todays could stand some improvement too."

Torey smiled. "You know, Ashley, you complain a lot, but you never give us specifics," she said. "Just what is so bad about life in Ashley, Missouri?"

Robin was glad they'd gotten off the subject of Caro. She wasn't in the habit of blurting out things about her sister. Of course, back home, everybody knew everything there was to know about Caro.

"Are you kidding?" Ashley replied. "That would take years."

"How about summing up the high points," Torey said. "I don't think any of us really want to hear years' worth of complaints."

"Well, for starters, everybody hates my guts there," Ashley said. "I wouldn't blame them if they hated me for the right reasons. Like I hate their guts. That would be a reasonable reason. But they just hate me because of my name."

"Boone?" Torey asked with a grin.

"Ashley," Ashley replied, making a face at her. "It might be okay if it was a coincidence, but it obviously isn't. Think about it. They have to cheer me at football games. 'Go, Ashley, go!' 'Who's the greatest? Ashley's the greatest!' Cheerleaders all over Ashley have hated me since the day I was born."

"That's bad, all right," Torey said.

"And teachers never know what to do with me," Ashley continued. "They hate me too, but they don't dare show it, in case they ever want to apply for a loan at the old man's bank. I once had a run-in with my elementary-school principal, and the old man saw to it his contract wasn't renewed."

"He sounds a little overprotective," Robin said.

"Just of the precious name," Ashley said. "It isn't as if he likes me. All he really likes is money and power."

"What about your mother?" Torey asked. "Is she happy?"

"You really want to hear about my mother?" Ashley said. "This is the story of my mother. My mother fell in love years ago with some guy, and they got married. My grandfather didn't approve, but it was the one act of rebellion my mother ever managed. She got married to her Mr. Right. Only for some reason my mother couldn't get pregnant. My grandfather convinced my mother she had to bear him grandchildren, so she divorced Mr. Right and married my father, who is no great shakes of a human being, but belongs to the right country club. They had me and they stayed together for as long as she could stand it, which wasn't very long, and then she ran back to her daddy. And that is the story of my mother."

"So nobody is happy in Ashley, Missouri," Torey said.

"Nobody I know," Ashley said. "I think the truly happy people leave as soon as they can."

"This is sure turning into one morbid dinner," Robin declared. "How about if we start talking about something a little cheerier?"

"Like food," Torey said. "Food is always a cheerful topic."

As though he'd been waiting for them, the waiter appeared, carrying a tray with their dishes on it. He placed them on the table and then came back to refill their glasses. "The food's hot," he warned them. "Be careful."

The girls cheerfully ignored his warning and took healthy forkfuls of food. Soon the three of them were choking and coughing and pouring water down their burning mouths.

"The price of exotic," Torey managed to choke out, and in spite of the burning pain Robin knew would never leave, she found herself laughing and eating and enjoying life in a way she'd never known she could before.

5

WHEN THE READERS of *Image* fantasized about the exciting new adventures the interns were having that summer, they probably didn't include train rides on the Long Island Rail Road, Robin reflected as she and Annie found seats in a no-smoking car. But as far as she could remember, this was her very first train trip ever. Cars, buses, and planes she'd done. Trains were a novelty.

It wasn't especially crowded, and the girls had no trouble finding seats together. They put their overnight bags on the floor and made themselves comfortable.

"It isn't that long a trip," Annie said. "Forty-five minutes or so."

"I think it's fun," Robin said. "Much nicer than a bus."

Annie smiled. "It's nice of you to come with me," she said. "You really didn't have to."

Of course she did, Robin thought. Her parents had given her a twenty-minute lecture about how she had to be nice to Annie's grandmother and accept any and all invitations. Family was family, even if it was just family by marriage. "I'm glad to," Robin replied. "I like your grandmother."

"She likes you too," Annie said. "I'm glad it's just the two of us, though. I really didn't want to have to deal with Ashley and Torey this weekend."

Robin tried not to sigh. Torey and Ashley had declined the invitation in favor of a boat tour of Manhattan Saturday afternoon, followed by tickets to a big hit musical that night, and a baseball game at Yankee Stadium on Sunday. The weekend's events would be duplicated for her and Annie later in the summer, but even so she had to choke down a little bit of envy. Visiting Annie's widowed grandmother on Long Island just wasn't comparable.

The train started chugging slowly out of the tunnel. Robin eagerly awaited the time when there would be scenery to gaze at through the window.

"So, have you been enjoying it?" Annie asked.

"Absolutely," Robin said. "Haven't you?"

"Well, it would be more fun if I could eat," Annie replied. "I've lost three pounds already, though, so maybe this diet will be over with soon."

"I don't understand about that," Robin said. "You weigh what you always weigh. They must have known that from your photograph."

Annie sighed. "I had this boyfriend," she said. "We were together for almost a year, and then all of a sudden he decided it was over between us. I could have died. Instead I got really depressed, and just stopped eating. My food kept getting soggy from tears anyway; it was easier just not to eat at all. And I lost about fifteen pounds just from misery."

"And that was when you had your picture taken," Robin said.

"Exactly," Annie said. "I wouldn't have even applied for the internship except that it got my mother off my back. She was sure I needed something new to worry about to get my mind off Ted. Only then I found out I was in the running, and that made me so nervous I started eating again. It's amazing how fast you can put on fifteen pounds. I think it took me a day and a half."

Robin laughed. "So you got right back to normal," she said.

"I don't even mind weighing this much," Annie said. "Sure, I'd love to be skinny like Ashley, but I refuse to be obsessive about it. My mother goes crazy when she thinks she might weigh more than your mother. My mother is two inches taller; she should weigh more. But she doesn't see it that way. It drives all of us crazy."

41

"I love my mother," Robin declared. "And I love your mother. But the two of them are really crazy when it comes to each other."

"Are they ever," Annie said.

The cousins smiled at each other, and Robin realized she was also glad that Torey and Ashley weren't with them. It was good to have someone she could talk family to, someone who understood automatically. Robin had spent that week making explanations. It felt good not to have to.

"Did Caro apply for an internship?" Annie asked. "My mother couldn't remember."

"She thought about it, but decided not to," Robin replied.

"That figures," Annie said. "I couldn't imagine them turning her down. This whole business, it just seems so natural for Caro."

Robin nodded. Caro had always known what to do with success.

"I miss her a lot," Annie said. "I've been wanting to tell you that for a long time."

Robin looked at Annie. They had never really discussed Caro before, and she wasn't all that sure she wanted to now.

"Sometimes I think what it would have been like if it was my older brother who had died, and I just can't," Annie continued. "It's like the pain overwhelms me. And I wonder if you can ever be really okay about it."

"No," Robin said. "I don't think you ever really can be."

Annie looked thoughtfully at Robin, who averted her gaze. There were some ugly old houses by the railroad tracks. It wasn't much, but it provided a change of subject, so Robin grabbed onto it gratefully.

"Wrong side of the tracks," she declared. "Think we'll see Torey's house here?"

Annie laughed. "I think we're a little downstate for that," she replied.

"What's it like rooming with her, anyway?" Robin asked. "Is she always perfect, or does she make disgusting noises at night when the two of you are alone?"

"She cries sometimes," Annie said. "She goes into the bathroom and tries to muffle the noise, but I can hear her."

"What's she crying about?"

"I think she's homesick," Annie replied. "She writes letters to her family every single day. And she gets back lots of letters from them too. She must get three or four letters a day from her family and friends."

"Incredible," Robin said. "Oh, that reminds me. I have to call my parents tomorrow."

"Me too," Annie said. "I'd rather get letters."

"You and me both," Robin said. "It's funny that Torey's the one who's homesick. She's the one who's closest to her own home."

"Only geographically," Annie said. "She showed me pictures of her family and their home, and they're really poor."

"Well, she doesn't make any bones about that," Robin said. "I don't suppose she's told you why they're so poor?"

"Yeah, she did, sort of," Annie answered. "I don't think they would have had a lot of money anyway, but there was some sort of accident a few years ago, and it really messed up her family. Her father was blinded, and her brother was severely brain-damaged."

"That's horrible," Robin said.

"They refuse to institutionalize the boy," Annie continued. "He isn't a vegetable, but he's in really bad shape, but they refuse to let him go someplace where nobody will love him. And her father can't take care of him by himself, so Torey's mother can only work during non-school hours, when one of the other kids is home. And there aren't that many night jobs available in Raymund, so they mostly live on welfare."

"Torey must hate that," Robin said.

"Not as much as you might think," Annie said. "She seems more to accept it as a fact of life. In the summertime her mother works as a maid at the local motel. They need extra help in the summer. And Torey works after school as a cashier at the supermarket, and on Saturdays she works at the town's weekly newspaper. She does some baby-sitting too."

"And gets straight A's probably," Robin said. "And wins internships and looks incredibly beautiful all the time. She really is perfect."

"Well, she's a lot closer to it than I am," Annie admitted. "What's it like rooming with Ashley? I think she'd exhaust me full-time."

"She's better than you might think," Robin replied. "This may come as a surprise to you, but I don't think she's been homesick a single moment since she arrived."

"It's a good thing I'm sitting down," Annie said, and the two girls laughed. "So tell me about the editors you've been working with. How are they treating you."

The rest of the train trip was spent in sociable gossip. Robin couldn't remember the last time she'd felt so comfortable with Annie. Certainly not since Caro's accident. By the end of the train trip, she was almost glad her parents had forced her into these weekend plans.

Annie's grandmother met them at the train station, and after many hugs, divided fairly equally between the two girls, drove them to her house. Robin knew Mrs. Powell from Annie's brother's bar mitzvah and other Powell family occasions her family had been invited to, but she'd never been to her house or spent time alone with her before. The Powells always seemed large and boisterous to Robin, and therefore slightly intimidating. But sitting in the car beside Annie's white-haired grandmother, Robin felt comfortable and almost at home.

Mrs. Powell made a point of asking after every member in Robin's family, and Robin answered all her questions as thoroughly as she could. Then it was Annie's turn, and she too submitted to her grandmother's questioning. Then the girls were asked about their jobs and what the summer had been like thus far. By the time they were finished with that set of questions, they had arrived at Annie's grandmother's house.

"This is really nice," Robin said as Mrs. Powell showed her to her bedroom. "Thank you for having me, Mrs. Powell."

"You can't call me Mrs. Powell all weekend long," Annie's grandmother said. "I'd go crazy."

"What should I call you, then?" Robin asked.

"Annie calls me Nana," Mrs. Powell replied. "But you probably already have grandmothers."

"Two of them," Robin said. "Neither one a 'nana,' though."

I don't really think of myself as being one either," Mrs. Powell replied. "It was Annie's mother's idea. How about if you call me Sylvia? That is my name, after all."

Robin thought about it for a moment as she put her overnight bag on the bed. A week ago it would have been impossible for her to call someone's grandmother by her first name. But for a week she'd been calling all sorts of grown-ups by their first names, and it was always possible one of them was somebody's grandmother. "I'd like that, Sylvia," Robin said. "Just as long as you promise to call me Robin."

"I think I can manage that," Sylvia said. "Now, why don't you rest for a little bit before lunch, and I'll call you downstairs around twelve. How does that sound?"

"Wonderful," Robin said, surprised at how wonderful some time alone in a real bedroom sounded. She watched as Sylvia left the room, and then stretched out on the bed. In five minutes' time she was sound asleep.

"I took the liberty of inviting a few people over for after lunch," Sylvia informed the girls as they cleared the lunch plates off the table on the patio.

"Oh, Nana, you didn't," Annie said.

"Of course I did," Sylvia replied. "Listen to this girl, Robin. She gets upset because I invited one or two of my dearest friends to swim in the pool."

"And to show off your granddaughter to," Annie said.

"I should hope so," Sylvia said. "Someday you'll have a granddaughter, and you'll show her off too. If she's half as perfect as you are, you will."

"Nana, I don't feel like being perfect this weekend," Annie said. "I've had to be perfect all week long. I was really looking forward to spending a weekend just being normal."

45

"Normal for you is perfect," Sylvia said, and gave her granddaughter a hug. "But if you want, you can just sulk around and I'll show Robin off instead."

"No fair," Robin said. "I've been perfect all week long also."

"Oh, dear," Sylvia said. "I don't mind calling up my friends and cancelling out, because they'll understand, I'm sure. They have grandchildren too, all of whom, I feel obliged to tell you, are perfect also. But what about all the boys I invited?"

"Boys?" Annie asked. Robin put the dirty dishes down in the sink and turned to face Sylvia.

"Boys," Sylvia replied. "You know, those funny-looking creatures who turn into men all too soon. I figured at a magazine like *Image* there probably aren't too many boys around, and since you go to coed high schools, I thought you might be missing them. Unless they've integrated the Abigail Adams Hotel for Women."

"Not hardly," Annie said. "How many boys," Nana?"

"Four," Sylvia said. "One for each one of you. Only, just two of you came, so I guess that's two for each one of you. I hope you don't mind."

"I think I can learn to live with that," Robin said. "Who are these boys, anyway?"

"They're nice young men," Sylvia replied. "Neighborhood boys. Sons of friends. Each with a pedigree. I promised them beautiful young ladies and an afternoon in the pool. They should be here any minute now."

"Nana, you can't do this to us," Annie said. "You didn't give us any warning."

"So what would you do with warning?" her grandmother asked. "Go, leave the dishes, change into your bathing suits and have a good time. I insist."

The girls went upstairs to their rooms and emerged a few mintues later ready for a swim and boys. Robin reflected that after a week at an all-female hotel and a nearly all-female job, the very idea of boys was enough to make her salivate.

"I hope you don't mind Nana's little tricks," Annie said as the girls met in the hallway.

"I forgive her," Robin said. "Believe me, I forgive her."

"Four boys for the two of us," Annie said. "I swear."

'Annie, it's all right," Robin said. "Actually it's kind of great."

"Sure it's all right for you," Annie said. "But I've only lost three pounds."

"You look great," Robin informed her. "You look . . . What's the word? Curvaceous. Positively curvaceous."

"You mean hippy," Annie said. "Oh well. Maybe I'll dazzle them with my fabulous personality."

"Just leave me one," Robin said. "Whoops. I think I see some of them already."

The girls paused in front of the window and looked outside at the arrival of a carful of boys. "It's like Christmas," Robin declared.

"I'll take your word for it," Annie said. "Come on, let's meet our gentlemen callers."

Robin watched as Annie bounded out the back door and surrounded herself with a variety of boys and adults. Robin felt suddenly shy. She didn't usually mind meeting grown-ups, and in her life, she had never objected to meeting boys. But this felt different. Maybe because it was Annie's turf. If it was Robin's grandmother making such a fuss, she'd probably feel more comfortable.

"That's quite a crowd out there."

Robin whirled around at the sound of a strange male voice. It seemed to come from a tall brown-haired boy dressed in a bathing suit and terry-cloth robe.

"Hi," she said. "I'm Robin."

"The granddaughter's cousin, right," the boy said. "Mrs. Powell was explaining all that to us out there."

"Right," Robin said. "Only the granddaughter has a name. It's Annie."

"Annie," the boy said. "And you're Robin, and you're both interns at *Image* magazine. Do you like it?"

"I like it a lot," Robin replied. "Who are you?"

The boy smiled. Robin's knees came close to buckling. She didn't know where Sylvia found them, but if this boy was a typical sample, she could go into business. "Tim," he replied. "Timothy Alden."

"Robin Schyler," Robin said, offering him her hand to shake. "Pleased to meet you."

"Likewise," Tim said with mock formality. "I hope I'm not keeping you from joining your friends out there."

"They're not my friends," Robin said. "I mean, I don't know any of them except for the Powells, and I really wouldn't mind letting the crowd thin down before making my entrance."

"Good," Tim said. "I don't mind waiting either. How about starting with your life story?"

"It's been a short life up until now," Robin said. "I'm sixteen, I live in Ohio, and I'm spending the summer in New York. How about you?"

"I'm seventeen, I live three houses down, and I'm spending the summer in New York also," Tim said.

"New York State, you mean," Robin said.

"No, the city," Tim replied. "My parents are divorced. My mother gets me during the school year out here, and I'm Dad's for the summer. When I want, I spend weekends here during the summer, but that's my choice. I'm glad I chose to this weekend."

"I'm glad too," Robin said. They didn't make them like Tim in Elmsford, Ohio.

"Let's sit down," Tim said. "We're both dry. We can use the living room."

Robin followed Tim into the living room. It felt strange talking to a strange boy in a strange house when all they were wearing were bathing suits and robes. Strange, but not at all unpleasant.

"Do you like New York?" Tim asked.

"More and more," Robin said. "And how about you? Do you like spending summers there?"

"I didn't used to," Tim said. "But I think I'm going to a lot this year. Do they keep you very busy?"

"They sure try to," Robin said. "And we have curfews."

"We'll just have to manage as best we can," he declared. "Where's your hotel?"

"Seventy-fourth and Madison," Robin replied.

"That's not bad," Tim said. "My father's apartment is on Seventy-sixth and West End. It's just a cross-town bus trip away."

"Eleven on weekdays," Robin informed him. "Midnight on weekends."

"Any exceptions?"

"Only if you can prove you're my grandmother," Robin said.

"I'm glad I can't," he said. "You work nine to five?"

"Pretty much," Robin said. What if he decided she wasn't worth the effort?

But Tim smiled. "That gives us six hours on weekdays, and all day weekends," he said. "Even if we just spend from noon to midnight together on weekends, that's fifty-four hours a week together. How many more weeks do you have in the city?"

"Seven."

"Three hundred and seventy-eight hours," Tim announced. "That's a lot more than Romeo and Juliet managed."

"They didn't have to wait for buses, though," Robin said, dizzy with happiness.

"Yeah, but they wasted a lot of time with sleeping potions," Tim said. "Robin Schyler. What's your middle name?"

"Louise," Robin said, wishing it was something more romantic.

"Robin Louise Schyler," Tim said thoughtfully. "I don't suppose you believe in love at first sight, Robin Louise Schyler."

"I could sure learn to," Robin said.

"Great," Timothy Alden said. "I'll spend the summer teaching you the rules."

6

THERE WERE SEVERAL reasons why Robin was reluctant to introduce Tim to Torey and Ashley. For starters, there was the undeniable fact that Torey and Ashley were both better-looking than she was. Robin knew she was pretty, but Torey was a certifiable beauty, and Ashley had sexiness coming out of her ears. Robin had walked New York City streets with them and seen men's reactions. No point taking chances with Tim's newly minted affections.

Then there was Tim's attractiveness. What if Torey—or, far more likely, Ashley—decided he was her kind of guy? Robin figured she wouldn't stand a chance.

And finally there was always the long-shot possibility that Torey or Ashley would fail to realize just how perfect Tim was and spend the rest of the summer mocking Robin for her choice. Robin had a friend back in Elmsford who did that to any of her friends who started dating seriously. Robin had been the butt of her comments often enough not to invite the same situation where she had even less protection.

Annie liked Tim, Robin knew, from things she'd said on the train trip home Sunday. Tim was just fine for Robin, in Annie's opinion. Her grandmother's other three finds were also fine, but not for Annie.

"Nana refuses to understand I'm still nursing a broken heart,"

Annie explained as the train pulled into Penn Station. "I really loved Ted. It's going to take a while for me to get over him."

Robin muttered sympathetic noises, but already her mind was on ways of keeping Ashley and Torey from meeting Tim for as long a time as she could get away with.

She actually managed for close to a week. She arranged to have dates with Tim on Tuesday and Thursday nights, when the other girls were busy enough not to insist on going to the hotel lobby with Robin just to get a look. Monday and Friday nights Robin found she was busy and couldn't see Tim. Wednesday, it turned out Tim was busy. On the days when they couldn't see each other, though, they spoke on the phone for at least a half-hour. It had taken less than a week for Tim to become an essential part of her life in New York.

One of the things Robin discussed with Tim on the phone Wednesday was the planned Saturday-night party Mrs. Brundege was giving for the four interns.

"Please say you'll come," Robin said. "They'll supply us with dates if we don't have any."

"Then of course I'll come," Tim said. "They'll fix you up with some handsome Columbia student otherwise. I'm not taking any chances."

Robin thought back to that time not so long ago when a handsome Columbia student would have been her idea of heaven. She almost laughed at her foolishness.

"Just how formal is this party going to be?" Tim asked. "Mrs. Brundege is a bigwig, isn't she?"

"The biggest," Robin replied. "She's editor-in-chief at *Image*. But she also comes from this really rich family, so she has heaps of money on her own. And her husband is a partner at some huge Wall Street law firm. They have an apartment on Fifth Avenue that overlooks Central Park. That's where the party is going to be."

"So I don't show up in jeans," Tim said. "I think I can dig up a suit somewhere."

"My mother made me bring a couple of nice dresses," Robin

said. "I don't know what Torey's going to do. I don't think she brought anything appropriate."

"She's the poor one, right?" Tim said. "And Ashley's the one that sounds slightly crazy."

"That's right," Robin said, feeling somewhat disloyal at agreeing to such awful-sounding descriptions of her friends.

"And Annie is the one with a grandmother," Tim continued. "And you're the one who's pretty and smart and drives me crazy."

"If you say so," Robin said, happy that Tim couldn't see her blushing.

"I sure do," Tim said. "So what time is this party?"

"We're supposed to leave here around eight," Robin said. "Us and whatever dates we can get. We're to go straight to Mrs. Brundege's apartment and have a good time. Then it's straight back here, probably by midnight."

"Well, I can think of more fun evenings," Tim said. "But my mother says if I expect to date successful career women, I'd better get used to this sort of thing early."

"How many successful career women do you intend to date?" Robin asked.

"One," Tim said. "Robin Louise Schyler."

"That's more like it," Robin said. "See you tomorrow?"

"At five-oh-one," Tim replied. "Until ten-fifty-nine."

Robin spent the next few days worrying about what Tim would think of Ashley and Torey and what Ashley and Torey would think of Tim, and what the party would be like, and if her dress was appropriate, and all kinds of other things that drove her close to crazy when she allowed them to. On the whole, it was one of the very best weeks of her life.

Saturday afternoon the girls gathered in Annie's and Torey's room to see what they could do about Torey's wardrobe. Torey seemed to be the least concerned, but Ashley had decided that dressing Torey for the party was a worthwhile project. Ashley ransacked Torey's closet as the other girls looked on.

"This is pathetic," Ashley announced as she finished her search. "Where do you get your clothes, anyway, Torey?"

"Yard sales mostly," Torey replied.

"There must be some very sad yards in Raymund," Ashley said. "The only thing you have that is remotely fancy enough for this party is this thing." She took out a sleeveless blue dress and held it disdainfully at arm's length.

"That's my best dress," Torey said indignantly. "My mother made me that dress."

"I'm sure your mother is a great woman," Ashley said. "But she has the fashion sense of a doorknob."

"Fashion sense is not big in our social circle," Torey replied.

"You'd better get this into your head right now, kiddo," Ashley said. "This is your social circle. We are your social circle, for this summer, and probably for most of the rest of your life. Mrs. Brundege is your social circle. You're going to be kissing Raymund, New York, good-bye real soon, and you are not going to get too far in rags like this."

"This is not a rag," Torey said. Robin got the feeling she was actually angry.

" 'Rag' is a fashion term," Annie said. "It just means clothes—right, Ashley?"

"Right," Ashley muttered. She had returned to Torey's closet for a second look.

"There's nothing more in there," Torey said. "Look, I'll wear my blue dress. I don't see what's the matter with it anyway."

"It's drab," Ashley said. "It's childish looking. It won't do a thing for your figure. And it's stained."

"It is?" Torey asked, and immediately grabbed the dress to check it out. Robin looked over her shoulder. Sure enough, there was a small dark stain near the bottom of the skirt.

"Nobody'll look that far down," Torey said. "If they do, they deserve to see a stain."

"If you weren't three inches taller than the rest of us, we might be able to lend you something," Ashley said.

"I'll go out right now and get my legs cut," Torey declared. "Will that satisfy you?"

"What would satisfy me would be your letting me buy you

something decent," Ashley replied.

"I've already told you no," Torey said.

"How about accessories?" Annie said. "Doesn't *Image* always say you can dress up anything with the right accessories?"

"*Image* has never seen this dress," Ashley said. "Look at it."

Robin looked. It was pretty sad. Just a little blue dress with a high round collar. Robin would have killed her mother if she ever tried to get her to wear a dress like that to an important party.

"If we use really fancy accessories, then the dress will look even more ridiculous in comparison," Ashley said. "You know what we could do, though . . ."

"What?" Robin asked.

"We could rip it up," Ashley said. "Just a couple of strategic rips, and then it would look punk, and actually pretty sexy."

"We are not ripping up my dress," Torey said. "Do you really think I could carry punk, Ashley?"

"It would be a challenge for you," Ashley admitted.

"Torey could put her hair up," Robin suggested. "In a bun or a French knot. I bet she'd look like Princess Grace if she did. When she was Grace Kelley."

Ashley stared at Torey, who stared right back. "You know, I think Robin is onto something," she said. "Let's think of this dress as a classic and work around it that way."

"Torey has great hair," Annie said, already moving over to start playing with it. "My hair is just so horrible I can't do anything classic with it."

"We need a belt," Ashley said. "Hold on for a minute while I check my stuff." She ran out into the hall, and Robin could hear her unlock the door to their room.

"I hope Ashley isn't driving you crazy," Annie said to Torey. "Actually I hope none of us are driving you crazy."

"Just as long as nobody rips my dress," Torey said. "I have two sisters who get that dress when I'm through with it."

"It must be nice to be on that end of hand-me-downs," Annie said, continuing to play with Torey's hair. "I have these cousins who live in Newton, and they have heaps of money, which my family doesn't. My aunt is always bringing over bagloads of their clothes for my mother and me. It drives me crazy."

"Ashley means well," Robin said.

"Ashley means extremely well," Torey said. "How does my hair look up?"

"It looks regal," Annie replied. "Take a peek."

Torey got up and walked over to the mirror, Annie trailing close behind, holding her hair up. Torey smiled as she saw herself. Robin was pleased to see a sign of healthy human vanity in Torey.

"I do look good," Torey said. "Only I don't think I can really expect you to spend the party holding my hair up, Annie."

"I don't know," Annie replied. "It might be more fun than I'd have any other way."

"It's a very punk way to go to a party," Robin said.

The girls were still laughing when Ashley returned to the room. "I have it," she said. "You can thank goodness that Ashley, Missouri's idea of fashion ended in 1963." She whipped out from behind her back a white linen belt and a pair of short white gloves.

"White gloves?" Annie asked, dropping Torey's hair.

"I know," Ashley said. "Can you believe it? My mother still wears them when she goes to tea parties."

"Tea parties?" Robin asked.

Ashley raised her eyebrows. "They don't limit their drinks to tea, believe me," she said. "She's drunk as a skunk when she gets back from one of them. But she still insists on white gloves. And she made me bring a pair for all the tea parties I'd be attending."

"A circle pin," Robin said. "That's what the outfit needs."

"You don't have one, do you?" Ashley asked.

Robin nodded. "Circle pins are to my mother what white gloves are to yours," she said. "She wore one the year she spent in New York, so she made me take it with me when I came to New York. Circle pins never got out of style, she always says."

"She may be right," Ashley said. "Go get the pin. Let's see how this outfit works."

Robin ran back to her room and located the pin as fast as she could. By the time she got back, Torey was wearing the blue dress and Ashley was adjusting the belt. Robin tossed her the pin, which Ashley pinned on carefully. Next came the white gloves, and then it was over to the mirror to pin Torey's hair up in a simple classic knot.

"We're geniuses," Ashley proclaimed. "Look at yourself, Torey, and see if you approve."

Torey walked over to the room's full-length mirror and checked herself out carefully. "Should I be wearing sneakers?" she asked.

"They're a nice touch," Ashley said. "But they're probably a little too subtle for our audience. We're the same shoe size. I have a pair of white pumps that'll be perfect."

"I don't feel like me," Torey said. "How do I look to the rest of you?"

"You look beautiful," Annie said. "Like you stepped out of the pages of *Vogue* twenty-five years ago."

Robin began to hate the party dress she was planning to wear. She'd never thought about wearing a classic before.

"You'll outshine us all," Ashley said. "Except maybe me, but that's only because I intend to show a lot of flair tonight."

"I don't intend to show anything," Annie said. "Except that I've lost five pounds since I got to New York."

"That's great," Torey said.

Robin reflected miserably that she'd probably put five pounds on since her arrival. She was fat and flairless and definitely not classically beautiful. What could Tim possibly see in her?

She felt awful all afternoon long, and hardly touched her supper. Even showering and preparing for the party failed to lighten her mood. She finished a half-hour early, and Ashley hadn't even begun to change.

"Aren't you going?" Robin asked as she emerged from the bathroom.

"Of course I am," Ashley said. "I just want to make sure to keep my date waiting."

"Date?" Robin said. "You didn't mention anything about a date."

"I don't tell you everything," Ashley said. "You through with the bathroom?"

"All finished," Robin said, checking herself over in the mirror. Tim had decided to come a little early so they could have a few minutes without the others in the lobby. Robin stared at herself and tried to see the pretty girl she usually found there. She was probably lurking around somewhere, but Robin seemed to have misplaced her.

"You look great," Ashley called out from the bathroom. "New York City is lucky to have us."

"If you say so," Robin said. "I'm going downstairs to wait for Tim."

"I can't wait to meet him," Ashley said. "See you down there in a half-hour or so."

"Okay," Robin said, and left the room. She felt heavy-hearted as the elevator took her down to the lobby. How could she dream that Tim would still be interested in her when he met the other girls?

As the elevator doors closed behind her, Robin noticed Tim entering the hotel lobby. He was dressed in a gray summer suit and was wearing a maroon tie she could just tell he'd borrowed from his father. He was the handsomest boy she'd ever seen in her whole life, and in spite of herself she smiled with joy just at the sight of him.

Tim spotted her and smiled back. Robin rushed to him, and he started walking rapidly over to her. Before she knew it, they were embracing smack in the middle of the lobby of the Abigail Adams Hotel for Women.

"You're beautiful," Tim said, sounding almost surprised.

"I am, aren't I?" Robin said. "How do you like the dress?"

"It looks great on you," Tim said. "How do I look? Am I presentable?"

"You're wonderful," Robin said, and took his hand. They walked together to a pair of chairs and sat down to wait for the others.

Annie and Torey came down together. Robin had a moment

of anxiety, which was almost immediately washed away by an intense sense of pride. Torey looked magnificent, and she'd helped. Annie looked thinner and very pretty. And Tim was simply perfection.

They stood around chatting until Annie pointed out a strange-looking guy standing by the lobby desk. "He asked for Ashley," Annie said. "I heard him."

"She said she had a date," Robin reported.

Torey grinned. "It figures Ashley would find somebody a little different to go out with," she said. "Let's go over and say hello."

Robin and the others followed Torey over to the guy. Close up, he was even scarier than he had been at a distance. His hair was in the shortest crew cut she'd ever seen, and his eyebrows seemed to have been shaved off. Instead he'd penciled in upside-down V's, which gave him a permanently quizzical look. He'd also penciled in a large Z on his left cheek. He needed a shave too, although he smelled like he'd doused an entire bottle of after-shave lotion over himself. He was wearing a dirty white undershirt with a couple of holes in it, and exceptionally tight blue jeans. Robin decided against looking down at his feet, for fear of what she'd find there.

"You waiting for Ashley Boone?" Tim asked.

"I sure am," the guy said, grinning happily. "You all those friends of hers she mentioned?"

"We are," Torey said. "I'm Torey Jones." She held out a white-gloved hand for him to shake.

"Harvey Horrible," the guy said, shaking her hand enthusiastically. "Pleasure to meet you, Torey."

"Tim Alden," Tim said. "Is that a stage name, Harvey?"

"It sure is," Harvey said, grinning even more broadly. "I'm lead singer in the group Infanticide. Ever hear of us?"

"You know, I have," Tim said. "You play a lot of the SoHo clubs, right?"

"We sure do," Harvey said. "Actually my name is Harvey Goldberg, but Ashley insisted that for tonight I show up in my stage persona. A girl that beautiful, you don't argue with."

"I see you've all met," Ashley said, walking over to them. Robin hadn't even noticed her enter the lobby. And Ashley usually succeeded in making an appearance. "Well, are we ready to go?"

"As ready as we'll ever be," Torey said. "That's quite an outfit, Ashley."

"Thank you," Ashley said. "I thought it would make a nice contrast with your dress."

"It certainly does," Torey said.

Robin stared at Ashley. All she appeared to have on was a man-sized violet-colored sweatshirt with its sleeves torn off. What should have been its waistband formed a sort of skirt right below Ashley's crotch. On the shirt's back were large white letters saying NYU. The only other thing she had on were bright red high-heeled shoes. She'd put her hair up in braids, held together with very red ribbons. She managed to look simultaneously perky and perverse.

"It's all right, Robin," Ashley said, staring straight at Robin's gaping mouth. "I'm decent. I have underpants on. I am a fashion statement."

Robin managed to close her mouth.

"Well, come on, everybody," Ashley said. "It's time for us to storm the Emerald City."

7

IT DIDN'T SURPRISE Robin that the job she liked best at *Image* was helping out at the studio with Herb. At first he'd scared her a little, with his grouchy disposition, but after two weeks she found she got along with him fine if she kept quiet and listened to what he had to say. What he said usually interested her, so that was no problem. Herb had done fashion photography, but had given it up years before. "When models started having brains," he explained to Robin as she moved some of the smaller lights around the studio for him. "Used to be a good model was tall and skinny and brainless. Young and scared at first, and then a little bit cocky, but never too smart. Nice girls. They all came from the Midwest, like you, kid, and all they wanted was a little glamour and then marriage to a nice hubby, a couple of kids, and their memories."

"Sounds boring," Robin declared, lugging a light. "Sounds like they were boring."

"Were they ever," Herb replied. "Boring, but very well-behaved. Nowadays, they all go to college, and half of them think they know more about photography than the photographer does. Some of them are even right. And they know if they take care of themselves, their careers don't have to end when they turn twenty-five. They can market themselves for years and years. Big money. Poof, they're a corporation. I have enough problems in life. I don't need to take pictures of a corporation."

"So you take pictures of food instead," Robin said. Her arms felt like they were going to fall off.

"Food never talks back," Herb said. "You don't bite it, it don't bite you."

"But don't you miss the excitement of fashion photography?" Robin asked. "There's more to life than asparagus."

"Wait until they send you out on a location shoot," Herb said. "Give you a taste of that excitement. Then ask me that question."

"Do you really think they'll send me out?" Robin asked.

"Sure," Herb replied. "Don't think they don't come around asking me how your work is. They ask, and I tell them. You're okay, I say. You could use a little more upper-arm strength, but you're smart enough, and you got good manners. Your parents did a good job with you."

"Thank you," Robin said. "I'll tell them you said so."

"One thing to watch for when they shoot on location," Herb began. "The models are all well and good, but what counts is the clothes. Clothes in action. A good fashion photograher knows that, but makes sure the model doesn't."

"I'll watch for that," Robin said. "Thank you."

The phone rang. Herb gestured that Robin should answer it, so she did. "Hello?" she heard. "Robin Schyler?"

"Speaking," Robin said, feeling very grown-up.

"Jean Kingman here," the voice said. "We have an unexpected visitor here, and we'd appreciate it if you took a few minutes to talk to her."

"Sure," Robin said, although she would have preferred to keep talking to Herb. "Who?"

"Her name is Terri Antonelli," Jean replied. "She's the youth editor of the McKinley *Sentinel*, in McKinley, New Jersey. She'd love to interview you."

"Oh, okay," Robin said. "I'll be over in a couple of minutes." She hung up the phone and told Herb where she was going.

"Media star," Herb grumbled, not even looking up as Robin left the studio.

Robin walked rapidly down the hallways until she found Jean's office. After two weeks, she could find her way around *Image* pretty well, but there were still a few corridors that confused her. The smell of the test kitchen greeted her as she made her turns, but she steadfastly ignored them. Their makeover sessions weren't that many weeks away, and Robin had no intention of showing up for hers with a double chin.

"Here she is," Jean said as Robin opened the door. "Robin, this is Terri. Terri, this is Robin Schyler. Robin is our photography intern. She's from Ohio, and like our other interns, she's been here for two weeks."

"It's nice to meet you," Robin said, walking over to Terri and shaking her hand, picturing the way Torey would do it. Terri, she was pleased to note, looked impressed.

"I'll leave you girls to yourselves for a while," Jean declared, getting up from her desk. "But don't worry, Terri. I'll be back before you go, in case you have any questions for me."

"Thank you," Terri said. She and Robin watched Jean leave the office. "She's very nice," Terri said to Robin when they were alone.

"She is," Robin agreed. "Everybody at *Image* has been terrific to us. They've all made special efforts to make us feel comfortable."

"So you like it here?" Terri asked.

"I love it," Robin replied.

Terri sighed. "I was afraid you'd say that," she said. "I applied for the writing internship. I made it past the first cut, but some other girl got it. I was really kind of hoping you'd tell me I wasn't missing anything."

"Torey Jones is the writing intern," Robin said. "You shouldn't feel bad about coming in second to her. The rest of us have been coming in second to her all summer."

"She's really special, huh?" Terri said.

"She's beautiful for starters," Robin replied. "And she's obviously very smart. But it's more than that. She has so much self-assurance. I'm sure she's the one they'll use as the cover girl."

"That makes me feel a little bit better," Terri said. "But how about telling me all the stuff you *don't* like here? There must be something."

"Well, there isn't very much privacy," Robin said. "I share a hotel room with Ashley Boone—she's the fashion intern—and even though she's awfully thin, she takes up a lot of space somehow. And they keep you incredibly busy. There's the job, for one thing, and then they want to make sure you're never bored, so they schedule you for all kinds of evening activities. I've been to New York before, but there's still lots of stuff I'd like to do, and I know I won't have the chance to do most of it."

"Any other bad stuff?" Terri asked.

"Not that I can think of," Robin said. "I'm really having the time of my life."

"I figured as much," Terri said. "Oh, well. What kinds of things do they make you do, anyway? During your spare time, that is."

"We go to the theater," Robin replied. "And to museums. I can't get over how many museums New York City has. And we sightsee and eat out. Boy, do we ever eat out. The food here is fabulous. I may never eat in a fast-food joint again."

"Are there parties too?" Terri asked. "I bet there are parties."

"There sure are," Robin said. "Just last Saturday night, Mrs. Brundege, the editor-in-chief, gave a party in our honor."

"What was that like?" Terri asked. "Was it wonderful?"

What was it like? Robin thought to herself. How could she begin to describe what that evening had been like?

First there was the immediate camaraderie the six of them had felt. They'd laughed together from the moment they left the hotel until the time they got off the elevator at Mrs. Brundege's penthouse.

And then there was the reaction they got when the people at the party first saw them. It was great being part of a group that was actually gasped at. It was even greater knowing they weren't gasping at you.

Harvey was a big hit with the makeup editor, who rushed over to him and examined his eyebrows for what seemed like hours. She was intrigued with his Z also, and Harvey allowed her to run her fingers over his face to feel what he had done. Apparently she was considering it as a new look for the makeup section.

But that was nothing compared to the fuss made over Torey. Robin heard at least three people whisper "white gloves" as Torey walked in. The fashion editor immediately grabbed her and started checking out her entire outfit, circle pin and all. Torey obviously indicated that Ashley had helped design the outfit, because she was brought over to talk with them, and the fashion editor seemed to be listening very carefully to everything Ashley had to say. Then the hairstyles editor joined them, and looked over Torey's twist like it was a revolutionary hairstyle. Nobody seemed to notice the stain on Torey's pathetic blue dress, or even that it was a pathetic dress. Torey had carried it off.

Mrs. Brundege had set aside one room just for dancing, and that was where Robin spent most of the evening. She would have been perfectly content to spend the evening dancing with no one but Tim, but Mrs. Brundege had invited several young men who could actually dance, and Robin found she danced about half the dances with them. The rumor was that they were friends of Mrs. Brundege's son, Ned, but Robin didn't care where they came from. None of them was half as wonderful as Tim, but she enjoyed being fussed over by a collection of good-looking New York City boys.

Robin wasn't the only one they danced with. At first about half of them went straight for Ashley and the other half for Torey, but as the evening rolled on, Torey spent more and more time with just one boy, which left the others free to pursue Robin and Annie. Not that Annie was doing so badly by herself. Robin noticed, not especially approving, that Annie was dancing a lot with Harvey.

Robin got more and more curious as the evening progressed about who it was Torey was dancing with, but there weren't that many chances to get Annie aside to ask her. But when Tim went to the bathroom and Annie wasn't dancing, Robin tried to satisfy her curiosity.

"Who is that with Torey?" she whispered.

"Who do you think?" Annie replied. "That's Ned Brundege."

"You're kidding," Robin said. "Mrs. Brundege's son?"

"Son and heir to millions," Annie said. "Who else would Torey end up with?"

"He's gorgeous, too," Robin said, staring at him while he danced with Torey. "It isn't fair."

"You're right," Annie said. "Torey deserves more and better."

Robin wished Annie would speak about her with the same sharp loyalty. She wondered if Annie ever did.

"You've been dancing a lot with Harvey," Robin said. "What's that like?"

"Actually, he's very nice," Annie said. "He's majoring in premed at NYU, and he's on the dean's list. He's only in the band to earn money for med school."

"His hair is gruesome," Robin declared.

"It could be worse," Annie said. "He used to shave it off completely. He only grew it back when his mother got hysterical because he'd been invited to a family wedding. So they compromised on a crew cut. He plans to grow his eyebrows back this fall."

"What you're telling me," Robin said, hoping Annie didn't hear the giggle in her voice, "is that Harvey Horrible of Infanticide is actually a nice Jewish boy."

"That's it exactly," Annie said, and to Robin's relief, she was giggling too. "No wonder I like him."

"Well, I don't think Ashley is into nice," Robin said. "So you might have a clear field if you wait a little."

"I hope so," Annie replied. "Harvey invited me to hear his band play, but I don't know how I'll manage that. He says their sets don't usually start before ten, and SoHo is a long way away from our hotel."

"You'll manage something," Robin told her. But before she had a chance to figure out what, Tim was tapping her on the shoulder, asking her to dance.

And dance they did, as suddenly a waltz was playing. Robin saw Torey and Ned first, a tall, graceful couple. Then Harvey and Ashley caught her eye, the prince and princess of punk, doing a fairly respectable imitation of Astaire and Rogers. Finally she saw that Annie was dancing too, with one of Ned's friends.

Robin rested her head dreamily on Tim's shoulder and let the music carry her thoughts away. It was a moment indescribable in its sweetness, crystal clear in its perfection.

"What was the party like?" she repeated to Terri. "It was the best party you can imagine. They even let us stay out an hour after curfew. I mean, who was going to argue with Mrs. Brundege about that?"

"You have curfews?" Terri asked.

"Miserable ones," Robin replied. "They really watch over us."

"I feel better already," Terri said. "Thank you, Robin."

"Anytime," Robin said with a grin. "Want to see the offices? I can give you some idea of what I actually do around here if you're interested."

"Of course I am," Terri said, and she and Robin started walking around, with Robin mentioning points of interest. She was surprised, and pleased, with how many people said hello to her by name. She hadn't realized how much a part of *Image* she had become in just two weeks.

Robin made a specific point of introducing Terri to Torey, who, although she was busy with some copywriting, took a few minutes off to talk with them. When Robin and Terri returned to Jean's office, Terri said, "I see what you mean about Torey."

"She's unbeatable," Robin said.

"Maybe I'll reapply for the internship next summer," Terri said. "Maybe they'll confuse me with her. Terri, Torey. It's an easy enough mistake."

"I hope you do," Robin said. "And I hope you get it. This is a great way to spend a summer."

"Just what I wanted to hear," Jean said, returning to her office. "How did the interview go, girls?"

"Just fine," Terri said. "I certainly got plenty of material."

"Have any questions for me?" Jean asked, sitting down at her desk.

"None I can think of," Terri replied. "Thanks again for all the time you took. And thank you, Robin."

"Remember to send me a copy," Robin said. "I've never been

in a newspaper in New Jersey before."

Terri got up and left the office. Robin wasn't sure whether she was supposed to leave, but when Jean gestured for her to stay, she remained seated.

"How did you enjoy being interviewed?" Jean asked her.

"It was fun, I liked it," Robin said. "You know, Terri had applied for the writing internship. I told her there was no way anyone would have beaten out Torey for it, though, so she shouldn't feel bad."

"As a matter of fact, Torey wasn't the first choice," Jean said. "She only got it when our first choice turned us down."

"You're kidding," Robin said. "Who was first choice? Wonder Woman?"

Jean laughed. "Just about. She was beautiful, brilliant, and black. Mrs. Brundege always likes to have a good ethnic mix among the interns. But she got a fellowship to study the violin this summer in Switzerland and decided to do that instead. Of course, Torey was a wonderful backup candidate."

"Were the rest of us backups as well?" Robin asked, still shocked that Torey had been.

"Hardly," Jean said. "Ashley was hotly debated, let me tell you. She was obviously a risk, but she takes a superb photograph, and the fashion sketches she sent us were so talented that the fashion people won and she was invited. And there were a couple of editors who were sure Annie would turn out to weigh more than she claimed. You get an instinct about these things after a while."

"Annie's been very good about her diet," Robin said. "She hardly ate a thing at Mrs. Brundege's party."

"I wish I could say that," Jean declared. "I'm going to have to work out at the gym every night this week to pay for my sins."

"What were people worried about with me?" Robin asked, hoping the question wasn't too bad for Jean to answer.

"With you?" Jean said. "Nothing. You were our only unanimous choice this summer."

"Me?" Robin said, sure Jean had mixed her up with someone else.

"Absolutely," Jean replied. "Herb needed a little convincing, but that was all. There were a couple of girls who sent in fabulous photographs, professional quality really, but we pointed out to him that those aren't always the easiest girls to work with. But he was the only one with even the remotest reservations about you. You were first choice all along."

"Why?" Robin couldn't resist asking.

"Your demographics," Jean said. "They were ideal. You come from just the right-size town near just the right-size city and you go to just the right-size high school. You're one of two children, your father is a doctor, for heaven's sake, and your coloring was so typical, it was ideal. The makeover people were thrilled with your picture. You give them the right raw materials, and they can do wonders with you. As opposed to someone like Torey, who, no matter what they do, she's basically going to look the same. You are the perfect *Image* reader, Robin. You're the person we put this magazine out for. I bet you're even a cheerleader."

Robin nodded numbly.

"Of course, all this is strictly confidential," Jean said. "We wouldn't want the other girls to suffer any hurt pride, now, would we?"

"I understand," Robin said. "I won't tell them."

"Good," Jean said. "Well, Robin, it's time to get back to work, alas. Are they keeping you busy in the art department?"

"Busy enough," Robin said, getting up.

"That's good," Jean said. "We have a lot of wonderful things planned for you for the rest of the summer. And do come to me if you have any problems."

"I certainly will," Robin said, feeling very, very dismissed. "Thanks, Jean."

"Thank you," Jean said.

Robin walked over to the ladies' room for a quick, fairly private cry. Jean didn't have to worry about her hurting anyone else's pride. Her own was damaged enough for the four of them. She wished Jean hadn't said a word about the other girls and especially about how and why *Image* had picked her.

8

"HAVE ANY PLANS for tomorrow?" Shelley Haslitt asked Robin on Thursday.

"Tomorrow night you mean?" Robin asked her. "Tim and I are going to a movie. Why?"

"I meant tomorrow morning," Shelley said. "More like five, six A.M."

"Just sleep," Robin replied.

"How about waking up a little early and helping us with a location shoot?" Shelley said. "Think you might like that?"

"I'd love it!" Robin said. "You mean real fashion photography, with real live models?"

"That's it exactly," Shelley said. "I know I should have given you a little more warning, but things have been so frantic I haven't had the chance."

Robin had the feeling that wasn't the only reason for the delay, but she didn't care. After almost three weeks of watching vegetables being photographed, she was finally going to get to see a real fashion photographer at work.

"Where's the location shooting going to be?" she asked, images of all the glamorous possibilities flashing through her mind.

69

Maybe the Hamptons. Maybe the Andirondacks. Maybe even London!

"On the steps of the Metropolitan Museum," Shelley replied. "That's why we're shooting at sunrise. The light's better then but sunset is a lot easier because you can spend the whole day setting up. But the museum only gave us approval if we were out before the crowds started coming, so sunrise it is."

"Why the Metropolitan steps?" Robin asked, hoping her disappointment didn't show.

"We would have used Central Park except for all the trees," Shelley explained. "You have to be so careful when you're shooting winter clothes in July that there are no trees or flowers showing. Steps are a lot easier."

"But why in the city?" Robin persisted.

Shelley laughed. "We don't have an endless budget," she said. "Do you have any idea how expensive these things are?"

Robin shook her head.

"Well, for starters, the models can earn up to two-fifty an hour," Shelley began. "We'll be using four models, two men, two women. Models get paid more if it's a coed shoot. Don't ask me why. And then there's the cost of the photographer—don't forget, we won't be using Herb—and the photographer's assistant. Then there are the security people. Off-duty cops, usually. They cost money too."

"Are they to keep the crowds from bothering the models?" Robin asked.

"They're to keep the crowds from ripping off the equipment," Shelley replied. "Then there's the cost of the Winnebago we'll be renting to use as a dressing room, and kitchen, and all-purpose hangout. There's even the cost of the food to consider. We can't afford a couple of hours' transportation time, so an in-city location makes a lot more sense. Fortunately New York has a lot of different locations to use."

"I never thought about all the different costs," Robin said.

"I should hope not," Shelley said. "We don't like our readers to be concerned with that sort of nitty-gritty."

70

Robin blushed. She still wasn't happy with the idea that the only reason she'd gotten the internship was that she was the perfect *Image* reader. She certainly preferred it if the people she worked with didn't think of her that way.

"Well, now that you know what exciting stuff you have in store tomorrow, maybe you should get back to work," Shelley suggested.

"Sure," Robin said. "Just one thing. What time should I be at the museum?"

"Four A.M. and not a minute later," Shelley replied. "We're hoping to start shooting before six and be out of there by eight."

"I think maybe I should go to bed now," Robin said. "I'll need my twelve hours' beauty sleep."

"If the models get the sleep, we'll all be in better shape," Shelley said. "Get to work, Schyler."

It was hard to concentrate on the suddenly boring tasks that made up the majority of Robin's workday, but she put aside all her fantasies and ran around doing errands for everybody else. Eventually five o'clock arrived, and Robin scurried out of the office and practically ran back to her hotel. She waited impatiently until she heard Torey and Annie return to their room, and then she ran over there and told them her news.

"Four A.M.?" Annie asked. "And you're excited about this?"

"It isn't like it's the middle of winter," Robin replied. "It'll practically be daylight already."

"Early morning is a lovely time of day," Torey said. "Especially in the country. I know lots of people who get up around then to do jobs on their farms."

"Up with the chickens," Annie said. "Thanks, but no thanks. I'm very happy that we're not rooming together, Robin. Be sure to tiptoe as you leave the hotel."

"I'll be quiet as a cockroach," Robin said. "I'll have to be, to make sure I don't wake up Ashley."

"Don't worry about that," Ashley said, sticking her head in. "You should lock your door, you know—it isn't safe for you to keep it unlocked like this."

"We're willing to take our chances," Torey said. "Robin's

71

going to get up real early tomorrow to go on a location shoot."

"I know," Ashley said, plopping down on Torey's bed. "We'll be sharing a cab. Assuming there are cabs at that hour."

"You'll be going too?" Robin asked. After a moment's thought, she decided that on the whole she was happy to hear it.

"I'll be assisting the clothes stylist," Ashley said. "I was talking with her all afternoon about accessories. I think I talked her into white gloves."

Robin thought about how she'd spent her afternoon. It certainly wasn't in consultation with the photographer. She didn't even know who the photographer was.

"I'm sure it's all very exciting," Annie said, suppressing a yawn. "But I for one am starved and want to eat my measly portion of fish and veggies. Anyone for supper?"

"Sounds good to me," Ashley said, and soon the girls were at the hotel's dining room, eating and talking, and feeling good.

As far as Ashley was concerned, it made no sense to even try to sleep that night, but Robin, remembering that she had a full day's work after the shoot, and a date with Tim that evening, thought it was worth it to get as much sleep as she could. So Ashley was banished to the bathroom, where she curled up in the bathtub on top of a pile of pillows and read a sleazy novel.

It took Robin quite a while to fall asleep. This was the chance she'd been hoping for, the one to see what fashion photography was really like. Maybe she'd do something so brilliant, the photographer would offer her a job on the spot. Of course she wouldn't take it, not until she'd at least graduated from high school, but maybe after that . . .

Robin pictured herself living in New York, learning the ropes, living in a fabulous studio apartment in Greenwich Village. Tim was by her side, of course, going to Columbia, so they could spend lots of time together. Soon she'd set up her own business, taking pictures for *Image,* and then *Vogue* and *Glamour*. Ultimately she'd have a show at the Museum of Modern Art, but that was unlikely to happen for at least ten years. She'd have been on the cover of *People* magazine several times by then, and profiled on *Sixty Min-*

utes. She and Tim would be married, and he'd be a lawyer or an architect or something equally impressive. Maybe a Broadway producer. She'd leave that up to him.

Eventually she fell asleep and dreamed all night long that she was awake and not able to sleep. It made for a restless, uncomfortable night, and she wasn't all that sorry when the alarm finally went off at three-fifteen and officially woke her.

Ashley was snoring gently in the bathtub, and Robin was sorry to have to wake her, but she did. Ashley vacated the room, and Robin showered quickly, finding it hard to believe that she was actually awake and doing things at that ungodly hour. When she went back into the bedroom, she found Ashley curled up on her bed sound asleep, so she woke her up again, this time less gently.

"I am not a morning person," Ashley muttered, but she stood up on her own and made it to the bathroom. Robin listened carefully for the sounds of snores, but heard only water running. In a few minutes Ashley emerged, looking almost normal.

"They really should pay overtime," Ashley declared. "Or let us go home at noon and stay away from the office on Monday as well."

"I thought you liked it at work," Robin said, staring at the sweater she'd put out. She'd probably need it now, and regret it from seven A.M. on. Ashley wasn't taking a sweater, but Ashley was prone to daring gestures, and maybe she regarded being cold as being daring. It was so hard to be rational when you should be in bed.

She finally wrapped the sweater around her waist, pushed Ashley out of the room, and tiptoed down the hallway. Before they reached the elevator, Robin heard Torey whisper "Have fun" from her doorway.

"That was nice of her," Robin said to Ashley as the elevator took them downstairs.

Ashley didn't answer. She'd fallen back asleep, propped up in a corner.

Robin woke her up for the third time as the elevator arrived in the lobby, and the girls nodded hello at the night clerk and walked out onto the deserted street. New York was completely different at night, Robin realized. It was almost quiet, very still, and slightly mysterious.

"We'll probably get mugged," Ashley said. "If we get mugged, I will definitely demand combat pay."

"The muggers are asleep," Robin said. "We're the only people awake in all of New York."

But as she said it, a cab cruised by. Robin hailed it successfully, and the girls rode up Madison Avenue.

"We're going to the museum to break into it," Ashley confided to the cabbie. "There's a fabulous El Greco that I simply must have."

"Get me a Rembrandt while you're there," the cabbie said as he sped through the streets. "And a couple of Monets for my wife. She's a sucker for the Impressionists."

"I'll see how much space I have in my bag," Ashley said. "What are you going to take, Robin?"

Robin stretched. "Queen Elizabeth's bed," she said. "Or maybe I'll just go to sleep in it, and let you do the robbing for both of us."

"Well, here we are, girls," the cabbie announced as he drew up near the museum steps. "Have fun, whatever you're doing."

Robin looked out the window as Ashley paid the cabdriver. There were already people swarming around, even though it wasn't quite four yet. The girls scurried out of the cab and up the stairs, splitting up as they found the people they'd be working with.

"She's here, Paul," she heard Shelley call out as she approached her. "Paul Driscoll, this is Robin Schyler."

"Pleased to meet you," Paul said, shaking Robin's hand. "She'll do fine, Shelley. Thanks."

"What am I doing?" Robin asked.

"You're going to be our stand-in," Shelley said. "Paul is Jessie King's assistant. He's going to take light-meter readings of you until we're actually ready to start shooting the models."

"Do I have to do anything?" Robin asked. "Move like a model?"

"Just stand still," Paul said. "And be patient."

Robin found herself at the top of the museum steps for what seemed like hours. After a while she had to shield her eyes from the sun. She also shifted from foot to foot, and yearned to be anywhere else. She felt foolish and conspicuous, and very glad she had never dreamed of being a model.

"Who is this creature of loveliness?"

Robin turned around to see if the man was addressing her. He certainly seemed to be. He was the best-looking man she had ever seen.

"Greg Lewis," he said. "I don't suppose I'll be lucky enough to be working with you today."

"I don't know," Robin said. "What do you do?"

Greg smiled, showing an extraordinary mouthful of teeth. "Just one of the models, I'm afraid," he said.

That explained his dazzling perfection. Robin squinted at him and wished she'd thought to bring her sunglasses. They just hadn't seemed relevant in the middle of the night. Not only was he perfect-looking, he also seemed to be in his late teens, or early twenties at most. Only none of the teenage boys she knew, not even Tim, were quite that polished. This guy positively shone.

"I'm not a model," Robin told him. "Just a summer intern with *Image*."

"That's even better," Greg said. "That takes talent. I don't think you've told me your name yet."

"Robin," Robin admitted.

"What a lovely name," Greg said. "How long have you been here, Robin?"

"About an hour," Robin replied. "My feet hurt. Don't you feel silly doing this for a living?"

"It's only until my acting career gets going," Greg said. "I'm up for a very big part on one of the soaps right now. The minute that comes through, it's good-bye to modeling."

"Good luck with it," Robin said, wishing he would go away, and the assistant would dismiss her, and she could meet Jessie King, and start learning what fashion photography was all about.

"Gregory!" a woman called out, and sure enough, Greg scurried away, leaving Robin standing all alone. Half her wishes were granted, Robin realized, but she still wasn't happy with her function in life.

When she tried to break away, though, Paul told her to get back there, since he had to do the final light-meter readings. Robin sighed, shifted, and squinted a few minutes longer.

Then out came the models, all dressed in perfect winter fashion. Robin nearly died from sympathy when she saw them dressed in wool coats and scarves. Sure enough, one of the women had white gloves on. What's more, her scarf was being held together with a circle pin. Robin knew she'd have to tell her mother that when she called on Sunday.

It was hard to tell who was the prettiest of the models, but Robin favored Greg, who was dressed up in a three-piece suit and a very fancy overcoat. He was sweating like a pig. Ashley, Robin noted, had been given the highly responsible job of wiping the sweat off the brows of the models. She felt better about her own job after that.

Jessie King came out of the van and checked things out with Paul for a few minutes. She was a beautiful black woman who looked completely competent. Robin was willing to bet she had great upper-arm strength, too. She'd definitely have to start working out with weights as soon as she got back to Ohio.

And then, almost without warning, the actual shooting began. As soon as it did, a crowd started forming at the bottom of the steps. It wasn't even seven yet, and already there were joggers out, and people walking their dogs, and people just out for reasons all their own, and they all seemed to have gathered around to watch. Robin was thankful she wasn't still standing in.

"Move a little to your left, Dorrie," Jessie King said, and the model followed her instructions. Soon Ms. King ordered the models to hold hands, laugh at imaginary jokes, play with their scarves, tease each other, and generally behave like four teenagers who'd known each other forever. She snapped pictures continuously, starting with Polaroid shots that took a minute or so to develop.

The pictures were rushed back to the Winnebago, where presumably the *Image* editors approved or disapproved them. Then Ms. King started shooting the real thing. Her assistant, Paul, obviously was keeping count of how many shots she was taking, since when one roll of film was finished he'd hand her a fresh camera and load the first one. He also handed her different lenses when she asked for them.

Robin watched it all, almost as fascinated as the crowd at the bottom of the stairs. Ashley was no longer wiping off sweat, and she too was standing to one side, taking it all in.

Then suddenly it was over. "I have enough," Ms. King declared. "Thanks, everybody."

"Thank you," Shelley said, and the models broke their poses and ran back to the Winnebago, presumably to change into something a little cooler.

Robin walked over to where Paul was putting away Ms. King's equipment. He was surrounded by security guards, but she was let through.

"Oh, Jessie," Paul said. "This is Robin, the *Image* apprentice. She was a great help to me all morning long."

"Hello, Robin," Ms. King said, smiling at her. "What did you think about all this?"

"Some of it was fun, and some of it just seemed tedious," Robin said. "I don't know yet."

Ms. King laughed. "That's probably true of any job," she said. "Have you been thinking of photography as a livelihood?"

"I've been dreaming about it," Robin admitted. "I'm not sure that's the same thing."

"It isn't always," Ms. King said. "All I can tell you is try every sort of photography before you decide on one. I used to fantasize endlessly about being a news photographer, going to war armed with a camera, taking pictures that would show the world the futility of it all. My mother, on the other hand, thought I should be happy taking pictures of weddings and babies. I ended up in fashion. Believe me, I never thought about fashion. I just stumbled into it, and now I love it and can't imagine doing anything else."

"So I should keep my mind open," Robin said.

"That's it exactly," Ms. King said. "Would you like to come to my studio someday this summer and see how it's set up?"

"Could I really?" Robin asked. "That would be wonderful."

"Here's my card," Ms. King said, digging one out of her bag. "Call me one day next week and we'll set something up."

"Oh, thank you," Robin said, not believing her luck. But before she had a chance to thank Ms. King more profusely, the photographer had walked away.

Robin stared at the business card and thought about the advice she'd been given. She was supposed to keep her mind open. That was no problem. The challenge, Robin knew, was going to be keeping her eyes open for the rest of the day.

9

"OH, PLEASE SAY I can."

"Let me get this straight," Herb said to Robin. He was obviously enjoying watching her beg. "Some bigwig here thinks you can be trusted to take a few black-and-white pictures of a TV star, and they want me to lend you a camera to do this?"

"Jennifer Fitzhugh," Robin said. "She's the star of *Highwater*. You must have heard of it."

"I never watch television," Herb replied. "I read books. You might try that sometime yourself."

"If I promise to read a book, will you let me use a camera?" Robin asked.

"I suppose you'll want film too," Herb grumbled. "A man gets a job, works hard at it, devotes himself to immortalizing cupcakes for the children of America, and what's his reward? Teenagers beg him for expensive cameras and film to play photographer with."

"You don't own the camera," Robin pointed out. "You didn't pay for the film. You're just in charge of them."

"Well, if you put it that way, how can I say no," Herb replied. "You absolutely swear to guard the camera with your life? I don't want to see a scratch on it when I get it back."

"It'll be scratchless," Robin said. "Herb, can I have the camera tonight?"

"I thought you said this fabulous opportunity was happening tomorrow," Herb said.

"It is," Robin said. "But I want to get a feel for the camera. I thought I might ask the other girls if they'd be stand-ins tonight, so I can get an idea of what kinds of pictures to take."

"That's actually not a bad idea," Herb said.

"You taught it to me," Robin replied.

"You're going to go far, kid," Herb said. "Okay. One camera tonight, and a roll of film tomorrow."

"Just one roll?"

"You mean you think you'll need more than that? Okay. Three rolls. Amateurs!"

Robin hoped Herb had enjoyed their little game. It was unlikely that he would have turned down her request, although he did have the right to, since he was in charge of all the photography equipment. But they worked well together, and Robin was confident that Herb would trust her. She hadn't been so sure that he'd agree to letting her take the camera the night before, though. That had been a gamble, and she felt good that it had paid off.

She called Tim and rearranged their plans for that evening, since she wanted time at the hotel with the other girls for her rehearsal. Tim agreed to meet her directly after work for a long walk and a light supper. The girls' makeover date had been officially announced for a week from Thursday, and Robin was determined to be as slim as possible.

Later that afternoon she ran into Torey in the ladies' room. "Aren't you nervous about tomorrow?" she asked. Torey would do the interview, while Robin took pictures. It was easily the most responsible job Torey had been given in their four weeks here.

"Should I be?" Torey asked, apparently sincerely.

"Not unless you want to be," Robin replied. She certainly would be, in Torey's place. But Torey always seemed to do things differently. "Are you going to be in tonight, or do you have a date with Ned?" Robin asked.

"In," Torey said, combing her hair in front of one of the mirrors. "I don't know what to do about him. He keeps asking me out."

"You could try saying yes," Robin said, washing her hands. "He's really great-looking."

"He's very nice, too," Torey said. "But I don't think it's fair to Mrs. Brundege if one of the interns is dating her son."

"I'm sure she'd let Ned know if she didn't want him to," Robin said. "Why can't you just relax and have a good time, Torey? Don't make an issue out of everything."

"You're probably right," she replied. "See you later, Robin."

"Right," Robin said, and began combing her own hair. Torey always seemed to get worked up about the easy things, and stayed far too calm about the important stuff. As much as she liked her, Robin doubted she'd ever understand her.

Tim met her in the *Image* reception room. He took the camera case from her, and they rode down in the elevator together. Even though it was hot, the idea of a walk through the park felt good to Robin. Sometimes she felt cooped up inside the office building all day long.

"How was your day?" Tim asked as they started their walk.

"Great," Robin said. "But tomorrow is going to be better. Tomorrow I get to take pictures of Jennifer Fitzhugh."

"From *Highwater*?" Tim asked.

Robin nodded. "She's in New York, and she's doing a fashion spread for *Image*. They're sending Torey and me to her hotel room tomorrow to interview her and take pictures."

"That's great," Tim declared. "You must be really excited. I know you've been wanting to show them what kind of work you're capable of."

"I just hope I don't goof up," Robin said. "Torey has nerves of steel. She didn't even seem to know she should be scared. But I keep thinking of all the things that could go wrong, and my stomach aches and I wonder why I ever agreed to do it in the first place."

"Oh, no," Tim said. "Not another one of those speeches."

"What speeches?" Robin asked.

"I really don't know how to say this tactfully," Tim began. "But sometimes, Robin, you put yourself down so hard, it just drives me crazy."

"I do?" Robin said.

"Yeah," Tim replied. "You'll mention how much prettier Ashley is than you, or how much smarter Annie is, or how much more competent Torey is. Or you'll start moaning about your stupid demographics, like you really believe that's the only reason you were picked for the internship."

"It might be," Robin said.

"Don't be silly," he replied. "There are millions of girls with your same demographics, and none of them got picked. *Image* liked your pictures. They liked your essay. They liked the way you looked. *And* they liked your demographics."

"I don't whine, do I?" Robin asked. "I hate whiners."

"It isn't like that," Tim said. "It's hard to explain. It's more like you keep waiting for someone to confirm that you aren't special, when of course you are. Do you have any idea what I'm talking about?"

"Some," Robin admitted. She found a bench conveniently free of bums and sat down. Tim joined her.

"Girls do that sometimes," Tim continued. "More than boys. Like it's good somehow to think you aren't so great, even if you really are. False modesty, I guess. It drives me crazy."

"But it isn't always false modesty," Robin said. "Sometimes it's genuine insecurity."

"What do you have to be insecure about?" Tim asked. "How can you possibly think you're inadequate?"

Robin shook her head. "That's easy," she said. "All I have to do is compare myself to Caro."

"Your sister," Tim said.

"My sister," Robin said. "You have to understand about Caro. She was wonderful. She was everything you could dream of in an older sister. She let me hang out with her, try on her clothes, play with her makeup. When her friends teased me, she made them stop. She was three years older than me, but she was my best friend."

"You must miss her a lot," Tim said, putting his arm around Robin.

"Of course I miss her," Robin said. "But that's not the point. The thing is, Caro was perfect. She got straight A's in school. She was always being elected president of her class. She did volunteer work at the senior citizens' center, and she won every award they had at our school. Everybody loved her. She was never nasty to people, or short with them, and even the jerks and the losers knew she cared about them."

"That must have been a tough act to follow," Tim said.

"But then she was in the accident," Robin continued, her voice quavering. "It was really so crazy. She was such a careful driver, just the way you'd have expected her to be, and it was all such a fluke. It was a dark rainy evening, and she was doing the speed limit on a back road, so she was going around forty-five, when a kid ran out into the road, and she swerved to avoid hitting him. That was so typical of her, to risk her own life rather than hurt somebody else. She probably would have been okay if the ground hadn't been so wet, but she skidded and lost control of the car and rammed into a tree. The kid ran to get help, but she was still stuck in the car for about half an hour."

Tim sat absolutely still. Around them, people continued to play Frisbee, jog in perfect rhythm, and use the park for their own enjoyment.

"The doctors operated on her all night long," Robin said. "They thought it was amazing she was still alive. She was a mess of internal injuries. But Caro wasn't going to give up living that easily. She made it through surgery, and then a few days later she started bleeding internally again, and they had to operate again, and she made it through that too."

Robin swallowed hard. "All that happened right before graduation. Caro wanted to go to graduation so badly, but of course she couldn't. She begged everybody, doctors, nurses, my parents, even me, but there just wasn't any way she could have gone. She was wired up, on IV and that sort of thing, and she was stuck in the hospital bed. But the kids in her high-school class wanted her there too. They even tried to convince the hospital that Caro should be allowed a ceremony in her hospital room, but the problem was, no more than four of them would have been allowed in, and even that was breaking lots of rules, and they couldn't decide which four should get to go. So instead they had the graduation indoors in the gym, instead of outside, the way they had originally planned, and they set up speakers and they called up Caro when the graduation began and she got to be there by phone. She heard everything, and she said a few words to everybody there about how she'd be seeing them all soon. She won two awards that night, and every time her name was mentioned, even when it was just time for her to get her diploma, everybody cheered. We didn't have a conference phone at our end, but it didn't matter, the cheers were so loud we could all hear them all over the room. And the doctors and nurses came in, and we were all cheering there too, and Caro was lying on her bed giggling away."

"She died soon after that?" Tim asked very softly. Robin was already crying. He found a handkerchief and handed it to her.

"Two weeks later," Robin said. "We all kept thinking if she'd made it through both operations she was bound to recover completely. We knew it would take a long time, and she'd have to have lots of physical therapy, but you could just see she was getting stronger. The doctors kept telling us she wasn't out of the woods, but I don't think any of us really believed them. They didn't know Caro. Caro wasn't going to give up. Not after she'd been through so much. Only she went into kidney failure and she got pneumonia and all of a sudden she was dead. Three days before, she'd been laughing and making plans, and then she was dead."

She paused for a moment, and in spite of the warmth of the day, shivered from the memory. "We had a funeral for the family only. But a couple of days later, there was a memorial service. School was already out, and a lot of the kids from Caro's class had jobs, but every single kid came. All the teachers did too. Every single one. Mom cried for three days after that. She just couldn't stop crying because everybody came. That's what Caro was like."

"But you're special too," Tim said. "Nobody thinks you're something less, just because you aren't Caro."

"I think it," Robin said, and blew her nose with Tim's handkerchief. "I think it, and I always will. Caro is the standard I measure my life by, and no matter what I do, I never measure up."

"Do you think Caro would want you to do that?" Tim asked.

"No, of course not," Robin replied. "But not even Caro always got what she wanted. When she swerved to avoid hitting the kid, it never occurred to her that she might die as a result. Caro never thought she could just die. Even when she was in the hospital, even between the operations, which was the scariest time for all of us, she never thought she would die. She was worried about being crippled, about having to start college a year late, about what the accident was costing. She even worried about the kid, and how he was feeling, and how Mom and Dad were managing without the car. Death wasn't a possibility at all until it happened. That was something not even Caro could control."

"I don't think any of us can really control death," Tim said. "Or life, for that matter."

"Exactly," Robin said. "So if I don't feel inadequate because I don't measure up to Caro, I feel helpless and out of control. Great combination, right?"

"I love you," Tim said. "You. Robin Louise Schyler. No matter how you feel about yourself, I love you, and I wish I could make the pain go away."

"It's nice that you want to," Robin said, managing a small smile. "But it isn't the sort of pain that ever goes away."

"It's a beautiful day," Tim said. "And you're in New York, and you're with me, and tomorrow you're going to be taking pictures of a famous TV star, and those pictures are going to be appearing in a big national magazine. Because those pictures are going to be perfect. Did I mention that before?"

"Not often enough," Robin said, snuggling next to Tim.

"Well, they are," he said. "You'll probably win a Pulitzer Prize for them."

"No," Robin said. "I'm tired of those fantasies."

"Okay," Tim said. "Forget the Pulitzer. It's going to be accomplishment enough that the pictures will turn out well and get published. And that will be something you did, Robin, all by yourself. We'll all be very proud of you, and maybe then you'll have some idea of just how amazing you really are."

Robin knew it would take a lot more than that. But she also knew taking the best possible pictures of Jennifer Fitzhugh would be a good place to start.

"Do you mind if we skip supper?" she asked. "I'm really not very hungry."

"Are you going to go out afterward and eat junk food instead?" Tim asked mock sternly.

"Probably," Robin admitted.

"Okay, fine," he said. "Then you can skip supper."

Robin laughed. "I think I'll feel better about things if I give myself a lot of rehearsal time," she told him. "I think I should go back to the hotel, find some willing models, and make believe I'm a big-time magazine photographer, at least for tonight."

"And then tomorrow you'll be one," he said.

"I'll sure give it my best shot," she replied. "Okay, Tim?"

"Okay," he said, and they got up and started walking toward the hotel. "You know, Robin, girls aren't the only ones who get insecure about things," he said as they walked past three jugglers and a mime. Central Park never failed to astound Robin.

"It never occurred to me they were," Robin said. "What makes you insecure? Your parents' divorce?"

"No, that's okay now," he said. "That's just part of life now. Not that I'd mind if they got back together."

"What then?" she asked, feeling better than she had in a long time. "School?"

"No, I do pretty well in school," he replied. "I think I'll be able to get into a good college somewhere."

"Pimples," Robin said. "You worry about your complexion."

"No!" Tim said sharply. "Should I?"

Robin laughed. "Absolutely not," she said, planting a kiss on Tim's pimple-free cheek. "I was just teasing."

"You should never tease about important things like pimples," he informed her. "Pimples and bad breath and dandruff. Those are not amusing topics."

"I'll keep that in mind," Robin said. "Sorry. So what does make you insecure, Mr. Perfect?"

"Girls," Tim said. "Not all girls. Just one. Just you. You make me insecure, Robin."

"Me?" Robin squeaked. "I spill out my guts to you in the middle of Central Park, and I make you insecure?"

"I told you I loved you," he said. "I called you by your complete name and told you I loved you. And all you did was cry."

"I wasn't crying about that," Robin said. "You know that, Tim."

"Yes, I do," he admitted. "But it makes me nervous when you don't tell me how you feel."

"You know how I feel," Robin said. "Don't you?"

"I have a sneaking suspicion," he said. "But I wouldn't mind if you confirmed it for me."

"I love you, Timothy Alden," Robin said. "What's your middle name?"

"James," Tim said.

"You mean you're Tim Jim?" Robin asked.

"No," Tim replied. "I can honestly say nobody has ever called me that before. Or ever will again, if they cherish their lives."

"I love you, Timothy James Alden," Robin announced. "I do, you know. I really do."

"You don't have to sound so surprised about it," Tim said, but he was laughing, and soon Robin was too, and they didn't let pocketbooks, or camera bags, or eight million gawking pedestrians keep them from a celebratory kiss.

10

"KIND OF PUTS the Abigail Adams to shame," Torey murmured to Robin as the two of them waited in the sitting-room part of Jennifer Fitzhugh's hotel suite. The room was twice the size of their bedrooms, and it didn't even have a bed, just luxurious living-room furnishings, including a nineteen-inch television. Robin walked over to it and patted it fondly.

"Her own TV," she said. "I'd forgotten how much I miss watching TV."

"I wouldn't know," Torey said. "We don't own a television."

"Who doesn't own a TV?" Jennifer Fitzhugh asked, coming out of her bedroom. Robin gasped. It was bad enough she was walking in on a private conversation. But it was so typical of Torey that it was one of those "we-don't-have" ones.

"These are the girls," Jennifer Fitzhugh's publicist announced. He'd been the one to let the girls into the suite. He was very Hollywood-looking in Robin's opinion, just a little too slick to be believable. "Girls, the incomparable Jennifer Fitzhugh."

"I'm pleased to meet you," Torey said in her best royal manner. She walked over to the star and offered her a hand to shake.

Jennifer Fitzhugh ignored the extended hand. "You don't own a TV," she said. "How come? You come from one of those fancy intellectual families that thinks they're too good for TV?"

"Hardly," Torey said with a laugh. "It's just cable hasn't reached us yet. And where I live there's no reception without cable."

"Oh," Jennifer Fitzhugh said, clearly mollified. "I guess it drives you crazy, not having a TV set."

"Well, no," Torey replied. "My mother always says you don't miss what you've never had."

"That is a crock," Jennifer Fitzhugh announced. "Isn't it, Ralph?"

"It certainly is," the publicist agreed.

"Why?" Torey asked. "What is it you missed before you had it?"

"Plenty," Jennifer Fitzhugh declared. "Like having a father around. He walked out on us when I was two, and if you're going to tell me I didn't miss having a father around, I'll tell you you're crazy."

Torey looked thoughtful. "You're right," she said. "And I'll tell my mother when I see her next. It must have been very rough not having a father."

"It was murder," Jennifer Fitzhugh replied. "Worse than not having a TV, I'll tell you."

"Jennifer's is a great story," her publicist announced. "Grit and determination have made her one of the biggest stars on TV, at the young age of nineteen. Her future is unlimited in its potential."

"That's great," Torey said, sounding almost sincere. "I was wondering if we could all sit down."

"Oh, certainly," the publicist said, and soon Robin found herself perched uncomfortably on the edge of a wing chair. Torey was seated next to Jennifer Fitzhugh on a love seat.

"Would you mind if I used this tape recorder?" Torey asked.

"Not at all," Jennifer Fitzhugh replied. "That way we can be sure you quote me accurately."

"Exactly," Torey said, turning the machine on. "Now, Miss Fitzhugh—"

"Jennifer," the star suggested.

"Jennifer," Torey said, and gave her one of her smiles. "Do you think there was some connection between your father leaving and your becoming a star?"

"Absolutely," Jennifer declared. "For one thing, it meant I had to go to work if my family was going to eat."

"Jennifer started modeling when she was just an infant," Ralph said. "She appeared in diaper and baby-food commercials, as well as doing a lot of magazine-ad work."

"Sometimes I think that's why my old man walked out," Jennifer declared. "He knew I'd be able to support Mom, so he didn't have to meet his responsibilities."

"Do you have any contact with him?" Torey asked.

"None," Jennifer said flatly. "He gave me a call when *Highwater* started taking off, trying to get on my payroll, but I turned him down flat. He wasn't there for me, I sure wasn't going to be there for him."

"What Jennifer is trying to say is that while she hopes someday a reconciliation with her father will happen, right now her life is too complicated to take such an emotional risk," Ralph said. Robin almost applauded.

"Thanks, Ralph," Jennifer said. "You knew what I was trying to say, didn't you?"

"I had some idea," Torey said.

"What's your name anyway?" Jennifer asked. "You and the quiet one hovering in the corner."

"I'm Torey Jones," Torey replied. "And that's Robin Schyler. She's going to be taking pictures."

"I assumed that from the camera case," Jennifer said, but she giggled. When she giggled, she almost seemed like a real human being.

"Robin's family has a TV," Torey said.

"Three," Robin said. "Three sets." It seemed like such a decadent number.

"And you watch *Highwater*?" Jennifer asked her.

"You better believe it," Robin replied. "My parents won't let my kid brother watch it, but he sneaks off to one of the spare sets and watches it on his own."

"That's terrible," Torey said. "Kevin shouldn't disobey his parents like that."

Robin wasn't about to tell Torey that she had fibbed and that Kevin wouldn't be caught dead watching *Highwater*. "I'll tell him you said so," she said instead. Torey could be such a pain.

"Kids should obey their parents," Jennifer said. "I mean, of course I want everybody to watch *Highwater*, but not if it means kids are disobeying their parents. I like to think I represent something to American teenagers, and that's the respect they should show grown-ups."

Robin suppressed a snicker. Unfortunately, she didn't suppress it well enough. "I'm sorry," she said. "But the character you play isn't exactly a saint."

"What is she like?" Torey asked. "I've never seen *Highwater*."

"Where do you live, Torey?" Jennifer asked. "The North Pole?"

"Not exactly," Torey replied. "A little town in the Catskills called Raymund. Lots of people there watch *Highwater*. I hear it discussed at school."

"What do you do if you don't have a TV?" Jennifer persisted.

"My father is blind," Torey replied. "So we read books out loud a lot. And we listen to the radio."

"Good heavens," Jennifer said, almost respectfully. "It sounds like you have it pretty rough."

"We probably have more in common than you might think," Torey said. "But I still don't know what your character does."

"What does she do, Robin?" Jennifer asked.

Robin knew a test question when she heard one. "Well, last year Lisa had an affair with her stepfather," she began. "Not by choice, but she did anyway. And when the season ended, she was implicated in the murder of Tony Rocco, who seems to be her father, even though she doesn't know that. I hope she didn't really kill him. I like Lisa. And the year before that, she broke off with her perfectly nice boyfriend because he didn't have enough money."

"That's not fair," Jennifer jumped in. "Her mother made her. Her mother is a real witch," she said conversationally to Torey.

"What Jennifer means is that the character of Marlena has had many difficult times," Ralph said. "Causing some severe problems between her and her daughter, Lisa."

"She drinks," Jennifer said to Torey. "And she's a real witch when she drinks. You understood that too, right?"

"I never had any doubts," Torey replied. "So Lisa has a real rough time of it. Does that give you a lot to identify with?"

"Lots," Jennifer said. -

"Of course Jennifer's family is nothing like the family on *Highwater*," Ralph said. "Jennifer is very close to her mother. She calls her every night she's out of town."

"You call your mother?" Jennifer asked Torey. "You do have a phone, don't you?"

"We do," Torey replied. "But I can't afford the calls."

Jennifer took Torey's hand and pressed it between hers. "You call your mother tonight. Charge it to my card. Ralph, find me my charge number, so Torey can call her mother tonight."

Robin sat there marveling. Torey had the most amazing gift for getting people to give her things.

"That really isn't necessary," Torey said. "I write home every night. And my family writes back. I know how they all are."

"You have any pictures?" Jennifer asked.

"Sure," Torey said. She dug through her bag for her wallet. "Those are my parents," she said, showing Jennifer a snapshot. "And these are my sisters and me. And this is a picture of my brother."

"What's the matter with him?" Jennifer asked.

"He was in an accident," Torey replied.

"Your father's blind and your brother's a cripple," Jennifer said. "Jeez. Some people in Hollywood think they have it so rough, and it's nothing compared to the way your family has suffered."

Torey smiled politely. "We're really all right," she said. "You don't have to worry about us."

"But I do," Jennifer said.

"Jennifer is known on the Coast for her generous heart," Ralph announced. "She's very active in her local Friends of the Animals chapter."

"Maybe I should start taking pictures," Robin said.

"Yes," Torey said. "That sounds like a good idea."

Jennifer continued to examine Torey's family portraits. "You should go into modeling," she told Torey. "The camera loves you. And you can swim in those cheekbones."

"Oh, no," Torey said. "I really couldn't."

"Why not?" Jennifer asked. "Your family could sure use the money you'd be earning."

"For one thing, I don't want to leave them," Torey said. "And Raymund isn't exactly the fashion center of the world."

"You're going to be leaving them someday," Jennifer pointed out. "You've left them already for this summer."

"For another," Torey continued, "I have no sense of what makes me look good. Sometimes I'll think I really look terrible, and people will come up to me and tell me how great I look. A model really has to know how to look her best. That's a real skill, and I don't have it."

"You have a model's face and figure," Jennifer said. "And you take a great picture. The rest you can learn."

"Why don't we start now?" Robin said. "Jennifer, do you think you and Torey could move over to those two chairs there?"

Torey obligingly got up. Jennifer took one final look at the snapshots and then followed Torey.

Robin positioned herself in front of the large window that overlooked the park. The natural light was strong enough that she wouldn't need to use a flash, which was a relief. She hadn't had that much practice with indoor shots, and flashes made her nervous. She knelt down close to Torey, so it would seem like Jennifer was making eye contact with the camera, when actually it would be Torey she'd be looking at.

Jennifer immediately became animated as Robin started taking pictures. She told Torey all about her work with Friends of the Animals and her own three pet dogs. She also reminisced about how she'd gotten the part of Lisa after auditioning for it with two hundred other girls. She discussed what it was like being a child model and a teenage actress. Whenever she was quiet, Torey supplied an appropriate question. How did it feel playing a character who was so obviously different from herself? Did she miss having an average American adolescence? What were her dreams for the future? Her greatest temptations? Her favorite ways to relax? She and Jennifer kept up such a high level of conversation, Ralph hardly had to say a thing.

Robin was impressed with both of them, but she was especially impressed with herself. Taking the pictures felt absolutely right, she realized. And it must have felt right to Jennifer and Torey also, since they seemed unaware of the clicks of the camera or the way Robin shifted position. When she knew she had enough pictures to satisfy *Image*, she sat down and let Torey continue to work.

"How about a picture of the three of you together?" Ralph asked. "Something for your scrapbooks. You don't mind, do you, Jennifer?"

"No, of course not," Jennifer said, getting up and stretching. "Get the camera, Ralph."

So Ralph got a camera of his own—a good one, Robin noted, although she preferred the one *Image* had lent her—and snapped some pictures. Robin and Torey posed individually with Jennifer, and also in a group shot.

"Give Ralph your addresses," Jennifer said. "That way he'll be able to send pictures back to your folks."

The girls told Ralph where they lived. Then Robin checked her camera equipment, Torey gathered up the tape recorder, and they both thanked Jennifer and Ralph for their cooperation.

"Please develop the pictures for me," Robin pleaded to Herb as soon as she got back to *Image*. "I'm dying to see how they turned out."

"You know I'm not being paid to do little jobs for little people," Herb grumbled.

"Think of it as a favor," Robin said. "A good deed. A way of helping a young person on her career."

"If I do all that thinking, I won't have time to develop the pictures," Herb said. "Okay, kid. Lucky for you, I'm a sucker for teenage girls."

"I'll wait right here," Robin said. "And guard the studio from invaders until the contact sheets are ready."

"Thanks," he replied. "That's very generous of you."

Robin grinned. She knew the pictures would turn out all right, but she was wildly impatient to make sure. If they hadn't, she didn't know what she would do.

"Robin? Oh, thank goodness you're alone."

"Torey, what is it?" Robin asked.

Torey entered the studio, carrying the tape recorder with her. "I have a problem," she said. "And you're the only person who can help me with it."

"Sure, what?" Robin said.

"The batteries were dead," Torey declared. "None of the interview came out."

"Oh, Torey, no," Robin said. "What are you going to do?"

"I think I can reconstruct most of what she said from memory," Torey said. "But it would be a big help if I could go over it with you to make sure I remember stuff correctly. And I know I won't remember it all. Can you give me some time now?"

"Now is perfect," Robin replied. "Sit down, and we'll go over it together." She felt enormously pleased at seeing Torey with a problem created by her own goofing up. It made her seem a little less perfect.

"First of all, what did she look like?" Torey asked. "I don't even remember what she had on. I never think to look at things like that. I can be so stupid sometimes."

"A blue blouse the exact color of her eyes," Robin replied. "Periwinkle blue. And white slacks, and open-toed white shoes. Gold-and-pearl earrings, and two gold chains."

"I don't believe you noticed all that," Torey said. "Robin, you're a lifesaver. Now, let's go over just what she said about her family."

So the girls spent over an hour, with Torey making frantic notes as they reconstructed Jennifer's comments. Robin noted that Torey remembered just about all of it, but she knew she was being a help in reassuring her, so she didn't mind.

"This is so funny," Robin said when they finally finished. "You won't care if I tell Annie and Ashley, will you?"

"Oh, no, please don't," Torey said. "It was Annie's tape recorder, and if she thinks it was her fault that the machine didn't work, it might really upset her."

"She's bound to notice the batteries are dead sometime," Robin pointed out.

"I'm going to buy new ones right after work," Torey said. "That way she'll never have to know. It was my fault, after all. I should have checked last night. But I was so excited, I didn't think to."

Robin shook her head. "Can I ask you something?"

"Sure," Torey said. "Why am I such an idiot? I was born this way."

"That's not it at all," Robin said. "Didn't you mind when Jennifer was going on and on about your family? I would have died."

"That was okay," Torey replied. "My family brings out the charitable in people. We're given turkeys at Christmas, that sort of thing. I'm used to it."

"But doesn't it bother your pride?" Robin asked.

Torey shrugged her shoulders. "I can't afford pride," she said. "Those turkeys come in handy. And I'm not going to become a model."

"I never said you should."

"You didn't have to," Torey said. "Enough other people have." She sat there, so still it took Robin a moment to realize how angry Torey was.

"Don't you think you should start writing up your notes?" she asked. "They're going to want an article to go with my fabulous photographs."

"You're right," Torey said. "Thanks again. And you swear you won't tell Annie or Ashley?"

"Swear," Robin said. "But for a price."

"What?" Torey asked. "Are you trying to blackmail me?"

"That's it exactly," Robin said. "I promise I won't tell Annie or Ashley if you agree to ask Ned to go on a double date with Tim and me."

"You win," Torey said. "But you should be thoroughly ashamed of yourself."

Robin grinned. Shame was the least of what she was feeling. Pride and triumph were a lot more like it.

It didn't surprise Robin, she was pleased to note, when she looked at the contact sheets and saw that most of the pictures had turned out perfectly. Even Herb told her they weren't half-bad, which was almost as good as the Pulitzer Tim had promised her.

Nor was she surprised when she read Torey's piece and realized it was close to brilliant. Jennifer Fitzhugh sounded just like herself, only slightly sanitized, the way Ralph and *Image* would want her to sound. There was no way a stranger reading the article would know it had been written by a sixteen-year-old amateur.

And two days later, when Torey's mother actually called and told Torey that Jennifer Fitzhugh had had a satellite disk and a twenty-five-inch color TV delivered and installed, Robin was hardly surprised at all.

"Just think of it as a giant turkey," she told Torey. "You can even name it for Ralph."

Torey looked at her and laughed. "There are times," she said, "times when I just don't know   " But she grew silent and didn't tell Robin what it was she didn't know.

Robin sat there and looked at Torey. Even if Torey found the answers to her questions, she'd be unlikely to confide them, she realized. And that was all right too. There had to be some form of pride even Torey could afford.

11

"BUT NOW NED'S sending me flowers!" Torey wailed. "See what you got me into, Robin?"

"My heart is breaking," Robin said. "An absolutely terrific guy is sending you flowers. Even Tim, who is perfect, doesn't send me flowers."

"If you hadn't made me call him, he would have just vanished," Torey continued. "They all do if you ignore them long enough."

"You have a lot of experience with this?" Robin asked, laughing. Only Torey would find it a problem that Ned Brundege was pursuing her.

"There have been other guys," Torey said. "You know how it is."

"I only wish," Robin replied. "Torey, I'm really sorry I can't get more upset for you, but why don't you just relax and enjoy it? Like your family must be enjoying their new TV set."

"Are you kidding?" Torey asked. "They hate it. First of all, Dad can't see what's on, so they have to explain all the action to him. And they get so many stations, and the reception is so good, all the neighbors keep coming over to watch, and Mom feels obliged to have something to feed them, and it's costing her a fortune. And they feel they have to watch *Highwater* and they can't figure out the plot at all. They just keep seeing Jennifer Fitzhugh and saying 'She's the one'—and they don't mean it as a compliment. Mom says the kids don't spend any time outside anymore; they're always stuck in front of the TV set. I knew there was a reason we never owned one."

"There must be something good about it," Robin said.

"My brother likes it," Torey admitted. "Which makes things easier on the rest of the family. They can just put him down in front of it, and he's satisfied for a few hours."

"Parents have been doing that with kids for years," Robin said. "Welcome to twentieth-century America."

"Maybe it'll be broken by the time I get home," Torey grumbled.

Robin smiled. At least she'd gotten Torey off the subject of Ned. Torey really wasn't much of a complainer, but when she did complain, it was always about good things. This was the third time she'd run into Torey in the ladies' room in the last week, and all three times Torey had been upset over something nice Ned had done. He'd asked her out for dinner. He'd asked her over for dinner with his parents (a thought, Robin had to admit, that would have terrified her too). He'd sent flowers. He'd called her at work three times. He'd done all the things most girls dreamed their boyfriends would do. And all he'd succeeded in doing was aggravating Torey. There was no accounting for tastes.

"Tonight should be fun, though," Robin said. "The Dan Keller movie preview. The four of us haven't done anything together in a while."

"That's because you all keep going out," Torey said, combing her hair. "You and Tim, and Ashley and Annie both with Harvey."

"Isn't that weird?" Robin said. "Has Annie told you just what's going on?"

"Just that Harvey is a perfect gentleman when they're together," Torey replied. "And she likes him a lot. What does Ashley say?"

"Not much," Robin said. "That's one of the things that makes me suspicious. Ashley never keeps quiet about things. Something must be going on."

"I don't believe this," Torey said.

"What?" Robin asked, reluctantly putting her comb away.

"The way we're standing around the ladies' room, pretending to comb our hair, when we're gossiping, and not working," Torey replied. "They aren't paying us to gossip."

"You're the one who started it," Robin pointed out.

"And I'm going to be the one to stop it," Torey said. " 'Bye, Robin. See you after work."

Robin watched Torey walk out, and then followed her. It occurred to her that Ashley might have told Torey something in secrecy, and that was why Torey walked out so abruptly. Ashley and Torey had made a connection, that for all of Ashley's endless chatter at Robin, she and Robin didn't have. And Robin had no doubt that a secret told to Torey would be a secret forever.

Robin walked back to Shelley Haslitt's office. It was unlike Annie to agree to see a guy who was also dating a friend of hers. Something was definitely going on, and Robin had the feeling that everybody knew what it was except her.

She was looking forward to the movie preview, just because it would be something they'd all be doing together. She missed the sense she'd had in the beginning of the summer of the four of them against the world. Lately they'd all been so busy with so many different things, they didn't do anything together anymore. They all had secrets. It wasn't as much fun.

And although none of them were admitting it, the fact that the makeovers were just a couple of days away was putting everybody on edge. How the girls photographed after they were made over would be one of the deciding factors concerning which one of them would be the cover girl.

Robin paused for a moment before she entered the office. She wanted to be the cover girl so bad it hurt. She was sure she wouldn't be picked. Torey was gorgeous, and Ashley oozed style, and even Annie was looking great, now that she'd lost some weight.

On the other hand, she reminded herself, she had great demographics. She was the perfect *Image* reader. Of all of them, she probably deserved to be on the cover the most.

"Are you going to stand out there forever?" Shelley asked her.

"Coming," Robin said. Fantasizing would just have to wait.

"This is really exciting," Torey said as the girls prepared that evening to enter the theater. "I never get to see movies."

"I never get to see good movies," Robin declared. "They only show junk in my town."

"I never get to see R-rated movies," Ashley complained. "My grandfather won't let me. I have to fight to get him to allow me to see PG movies. It's Disney or nothing, as far as he's concerned."

"I never get to see enough movies," Annie said. "I'd go every day of the week if I could."

"I didn't know that," Robin said.

"I love them," Annie replied. "I've been thinking a lot about it. Harvey says NYU has a great film department. Maybe I'll go to NYU and major in film."

"Look at this," Ashley said. "This theater is so cute."

The girls all checked out the theater. It was located in a midtown skyscraper owned by the company that produced the movie the girls were going to see. The theater seated about a hundred people, and the chairs were red plush, and, the girls soon discovered, rocked and swiveled. They found four together in a row they could all agree on, sat down, and watched as the theater half filled up.

"Do you think they're movie critics?" Annie asked as some of the people took out notebooks.

"Could be," Ashley said. "Have any of you been asked to review this thing for *Image*?"

The girls shook their heads. "You haven't, have you?" Robin asked.

"Of course not," Ashley said. "I'm in charge of creating fashion trends. That's a full-time job."

"I saw three editors wearing white gloves this week," Annie announced. "Only one circle pin, though."

"Fashion is an awesome responsibility," Ashley said. "But one I can live up to."

"Such courage," Torey muttered. The girls giggled.

"Behave yourselves," Ashley said sharply. "We're here as representatives of *Image*, and you know what that means."

"Do we ever," Annie said with a sigh.

"Shush," Robin said. "The movie is about to start."

Everyone in the theater quieted down as the lights dimmed and the film began. Robin settled into her chair and waited to be entertained. Movies were a special treat for her, and she really liked Dan Keller, one of the best and handsomest of the new young actors.

Other than the name of the movie, *Time Tomorrow*, and its star, Robin knew nothing about the film, which also added to the fun. The few movies she got to see, she always felt like she knew, because she'd heard so much about them already. This time she'd be the one in the know—unlike the mystery-triangle story of Ashley/Annie/Harvey.

Robin laughed at herself. Here she was, going to the preview of a movie, and all she could think about were the romantic complications that surrounded her. Romance could wait an evening.

"I wish I had popcorn," Ashley whispered. Annie elbowed her, and the girls had to suppress their giggles. This was going to be wonderful, Robin realized. A brand-new movie with brand-new friends.

Ashley sighed lustfully when Dan Keller made his first appearance in the film, and that caused more elbowing and giggling, but the girls soon settled down to follow the story. Dan was a freshman in college, trying out for the football team. Sure enough, he made the freshman squad. But another kid on the team, a spoiled rich kid, kept picking on Dan, taunting him and challenging him. Finally Dan couldn't take it anymore, and agreed to a game of chicken with the rich kid. Dan borrowed his girlfriend's car, and the rich kid showed up in a fancy sports car. They both started racing toward the end of a cliff, only the rich kid managed to stop his car at the last second, and Dan couldn't. His car kept going, off the cliff, and the next shot was of his twisted and mangled body caught inside the car.

Robin managed to sit through a few more minutes of the movie, as Dan was rescued from the wreck and raced to the hospital. But at the first shot of the intensive-care ward, she knew if she stayed there one minute more she'd get hysterical.

"Excuse me," she whispered, and started stepping over the others in an effort to get free.

"You okay?" Annie asked.

"Fine," Robin whispered. She worked her way to the aisle and ran to the exit. As she opened the door, the light from the hallway shone into the theater, and Robin slammed it shut as fast as she could, embarrassed by the noise it made. But she had to get out, away from that movie, before there were too many memories of Caro to deal with.

Robin found the ladies' room, and was relieved to see it was empty. She sat down on the cool tile floor and tried so hard not to cry she was almost surprised to feel the tears on her cheeks.

Why Caro? Of all the teenagers in America, in the world, why did Caro have to be the one to die? There were four hundred seniors in Caro's class. Why couldn't it have been one of them instead?

"Robin?"

"Annie," Robin said, wishing she'd torn off some toilet paper to use as tissues. "What are you doing here?"

"I was worried about you," Annie said. "And the movie was starting to drive me crazy, so I figured if it was bothering me that much, you must have hated it. I came to find you. Is that okay?"

"That's fine," Robin said, sniffling.

"I have tissues," Annie said. "I always carry a packet with me. My mother makes me." She dug through her pocketbook until she found them.

Robin took one and blew her nose gratefully. Aunt Gail was a smart woman. "You love movies," she said when she was feeling more capable of conversation. "Don't you want to go back?"

"Not unless you want me to," Annie replied.

"No," Robin said. "I really don't want to be alone right now."

"Good," Annie said, and sat down on the floor next to her cousin. "I dread going back in there. When I left, Dan had just found out he was going to be a quadriplegic. Half the audience is sobbing. Even Torey is sniffling."

"What's Ashley doing?" Robin asked.

"What do you think?" Annie replied. "She's snickering away. I think we're stuck with Dan Keller imitations for the rest of the summer. Go wash your face with cold water. You'll feel better."

Robin got up and splashed water on her face. Annie was right. It did make her feel better.

"We should talk about Caro someday," Annie said.

"We should," Robin said. "But not right now."

"We should talk about what her accident did to us," Annie said. "We were really close when we were kids. You've always been my favorite cousin."

"You were mine too," Robin replied.

"When Caro died, I got the feeling you didn't like me so much anymore," Annie said. "Maybe you resented it that it was your sister and not my brother who died."

"No," Robin said. "I didn't want it to be anybody I knew. That wasn't it."

"Then what was it?" Annie asked.

Robin licked her lips. "It's hard to explain," she said. "I guess I felt you let me down."

"I know I felt that way," Annie said. "I felt like an idiot. I didn't know what to say to you. I was thirteen years old, and somebody I loved very much died, and that made no sense to me. I was so angry. And I knew there were things I should know to say to you, but I didn't know what they were, and my mother didn't know what to say to your mother. My mother cried every single night for a year after Caro died. I asked her what I should say to you at the funeral, and she said I should say I loved you, but I was thirteen years old, and I hate to admit this, I was so embarrassed, I just couldn't say it. So I didn't say anything."

"You didn't even walk over to me," Robin said. "I was counting on you to sit next to me, and you sat way at the other end of the row. You totally avoided me all day."

"I'm sorry," Annie said. "I was thirteen and I was stupid, and you can't know how sorry I am."

Robin found herself crying again. She hated crying in front of other people, had hated it since Caro's accident, but now she didn't care. She sat on the floor sobbing, and soon Annie was embracing her, patting her on the back, and crying too.

"Oh, I'm so sorry . . ." Torey said.

Annie and Robin broke away.

"I didn't mean . . ." Torey said. "I mean, I'll just go."

"No, it's okay," Robin said, and took a deep breath. "Why aren't you watching the movie?"

"I hated it," Torey said. "I hate movies about accidents. Are you two all right?"

"We're fine," Robin replied, using a couple more of Annie's tissues. She wasn't the only one, she realized, who knew what pain felt like. "We're cousins. Annie and I. Our mothers are twin sisters."

"Is that what it is?" Torey said. "Ashley and I knew you were connected, but we didn't guess cousins. I thought you were old friends who didn't like each other anymore. Ashley thought maybe you were stepsisters who'd been separated. I don't know why we didn't think of cousins. Cousins is so obvious. You even look a little bit alike."

"We do?" Annie asked.

"Around the eyes," Torey said. "I'm babbling, aren't I? That's because I'm deeply embarrassed. I'm sorry. I'll shut up and go."

"Please don't," Robin said. "Sit down with us and help us change the subject. I've cried enough for one day."

So Torey sat down. Robin noted that even sitting down on a bathroom floor was a graceful act for Torey. "I don't suppose you ever had dance lessons?" she asked.

"Of course not," Torey said. "We couldn't—"

"—afford dance lessons," Annie and Robin finished for her.

"Now I really am embarrassed," Torey said. "I swear, I won't mention money again for the rest of the summer."

"I'm going to hold you to that," Annie said. "You should hear her sometimes at night," she said to Robin. "I swear she mutters dollars and cents to herself in her sleep."

"Ashley mutters boys' names," Robin reported. "Sometimes things get very interesting."

"I should hope so," Ashley said, entering the ladies' room. "I do it just to entertain you."

"Why are you here?" Annie asked, making room for Ashley on the floor.

"I didn't feel up to representing *Image* all by myself," Ashley replied. "Besides, the theater was being flooded by tears. What are you all doing here?"

"We're talking about who is going to be cover girl," Annie said.

"We are?" Robin asked.

"We are now," Annie replied. "I've been yearning to find out what you guys think."

"Torey," Robin declared. "Probably wearing white gloves."

"They aren't going to use me," Torey said. "I bet it's going to be Ashley. She's gorgeous. And what's more, she knows it."

"I admit I'm gorgeous," Ashley said. "But I've given this a lot of thought, and I'm sure they're going to pick Annie."

"Me?" Annie asked. "Are you crazy?"

"Not at all," Ashley said. "Think about it. Torey has an entire article to her credit, and they're using two of Robin's photographs with it. They're practically dedicating a fashion spread to me. And what does poor Annie get?"

"A good salary, fabulous times in New York, and a makeover," Annie replied. "That's enough."

"You get an article devoted to your diet, with before-and-after pictures," Ashley said. "You going to tell me they didn't take pictures of you as soon as you started at *Image*?"

"They did," Annie admitted.

"A big article about you," Ashley concluded. "With your picture on the cover. Wanna bet?"

"Sure," Annie said. "Because I bet it's going to be Robin."

"Me?" Robin squeaked. "You really think they'd pick me?"

"You're the prettiest one of us all," Annie said. "You're not beautiful like Torey, but you're so pretty. And you look the way *Image* thinks of itself. Wholesome and Midwestern."

"I'm not sure that's a compliment," Robin grumbled.

"I'm not sure it's a compliment to be on the cover," Annie replied. "But while all of you have been working, I've been looking at the last ten years' intern issues. And seven out of the ten girls they picked for the covers had Robin's coloring and facial structure."

"I didn't know that," Robin said.

"Research," Annie declared.

"Well, one thing is sure," Torey said. "One of us is bound to be right."

The girls sat on the bathroom floor and laughed. And when Robin realized she was laughing the hardest of them all, she only laughed harder still.

12

"I THINK I'M going to be sick," Robin announced as the girls sat in the office that *Image* had turned into makeover headquarters.

"I know I am," Annie said. "I can't believe we're subjecting ourselves to this."

"What's with you guys?" Ashley asked. "This is the fun part. New hairdos, new makeup, fashionable clothes to wear. For one golden day, we're the models."

"This is not my idea of golden," Annie replied. "This is my idea of being treated like a piece of meat."

"How do you feel about all this, Torey?" Robin asked.

Torey shrugged her shoulders. "I can think of things I'd rather be doing," she said. "But when you're invited to somebody's party . . ."

". . . you play by their rules," the girls recited.

"Exactly," Torey said. "So we might as well relax and let them have a good time."

"I'm going to throw up all over them," Robin said. "I just know it."

"That'll make a real cute cover," Ashley said. "How often have they used puking on the cover, Annie?"

"They've done some covers that make you want to puke," Annie replied. "Does that count?"

"All right, girls," Jean said, walking into the room. She was surrounded by *Image*'s hair, fashion, and makeup editors, as well as two hairstylists, and a makeup artist.

"Why do we always do this here?" the hair editor asked. "It would be so much easier to do this outside the magazine."

"You say that every year," Jean pointed out. "Mrs. Brundege likes it done at the magazine. She likes everybody to see the girls when the makeovers are finished, but before the photographs are taken. And there's no arguing with Mrs. Brundege, as we all well know."

"Big mistake," the editor replied, but the argument was already over. The first hairstylist to enter walked over to Robin and Torey, who were sitting next to each other. The other one approached Ashley and Annie.

Robin closed her eyes and prayed she wouldn't throw up. She then prayed she would disappear on the spot. Finally she prayed that she hadn't turned hideously ugly since the last time she'd looked at herself in the mirror.

"Not bad," her stylist said. "How do your two look, Rick?"

"I've seen worse, Jason," Rick replied. "There are possibilities here."

"Here too," Jason said, holding Torey's head up by her chin and checking it over.

"What are you going to do to my hair?" Torey asked nervously.

"I don't know yet," Jason said. "What do you want to have done?"

"Maybe you should cut it all off," Torey suggested. "I could use an easy-to-care-for hairstyle."

"No," Jean said. "We don't want that. We want long hair on one of the girls, to show all the different hairstyles possible with it."

"Shame," Jason said. "It would have been fun to give you a really short cut. Your bone structure could carry it. Oh, well. I suppose I could always chop this one's head off."

"That's *hair* off," Rick said. "Cut the *hair*. Leave the *head*."

"Oh, that's right," Jason said. "What's your name, dear?"

It took Robin a moment to realize they were talking about her head. "Robin," she said. "Please don't cut off my head."

"I'll try not to," Jason replied. "How would you like your hair, Robin?"

Robin tried to remember if Tim had said anything about how he liked her hair. She vaguely remembered him saying that he loved it, once when he was listing everything that was perfect about her. She had the feeling that didn't commit her to keeping her hair exactly as it was. "Shorter," she said. "And it waves a lot. A style that goes with the waves."

"That sounds reasonable," Jason said. "Any problems with that, Jean?"

"None," she said. "Now, what can Rick do with Ashley and Annie?"

"Miracles," Rick replied. "For this one . . ."

"Annie," Annie informed him.

"For Annie, some big waves," he said. "Great hair, but straight just isn't very interesting. Some bangs too, I think. Soften that forehead."

"Just don't soften my brain," Annie said.

"And for Ashley, something daring, I think," Rick continued. "You look like the daring type to me."

"The daringer the better," Ashley said. "I want to look like I've never seen Missouri."

"I'll start with Torey," Jason said. "Since all I'm doing is trimming her a little."

"And I'll start with Annie," Rick said. "It'll give me more of a chance to decide what daring things I should do with Ashley."

Robin and Ashley watched as the hairstylists cut the other girls' freshly washed hair. Robin felt like it took forever, although she knew it didn't. But everybody was so quiet while the men were working.

When Jason was finished with Torey's hair, he put it up in a knot, not all that different from the one Annie had created for her.

"This is a beautiful girl," he said, examining his handiwork. "This one is a stunner. Do you know that, Jean?"

"We have some idea," Jean replied. "Now, what can you do about Robin?"

"I can make her so cute it'll be frightening," he replied.

"Perfect," Jean said. "Go to it."

Jason took Robin to the dressing room and washed her hair. As they walked back to the makeover room, Robin's knees shook. Sitting down in the rented barber chair was an immense relief.

Jason started with little snips, and then cut more and more of Robin's once-shoulder-length hair. Robin hoped Tim had nothing against short-haired girls.

It was fascinating to watch in the mirror as her hair kept falling to the floor. Robin wasn't all that sure she would recognize herself by the time the haircut was finished.

Jason finished with her about the same time Rick finished with Annie. Robin wasn't sure which one of them was more transformed.

Instead of Annie's standard do-nothing hair, there were cascading waves. She had the slightest wisps of bangs that reached almost to her eyebrows. An always-nice-looking girl was now positively lovely.

"Wow," Robin said in honest appreciation.

"You don't look so bad yourself," Annie said as Robin examined herself in the mirror.

Annie was right. Robin looked terrific. Jason had blown dry her newly shortened hair so that each wave acted like it belonged there. Robin felt she was the living embodiment of "pretty."

"Now for Ashley," Rick said. "Something very deco, I think."

"Remember your market," Jean told him.

"The girl is all angles anyway," Rick said. "There's no point trying to soften this face."

"Nothing too daring," Jean said.

"Trust me," Rick replied, and took Ashley off for her hair washing.

"Why did you put so much makeup on me?" Torey cried.

Everyone turned to look at her. Robin had been so involved with her own haircut, she hadn't even realized the makeup artist had started on Torey.

"I didn't put too much on you," the woman said.

"I look painted," Torey said. "I can't afford this much makeup. What's the point of making me over if I can't afford to stay made-over?"

"You don't have to stay made-over, Torey," Jean told her. "As far as we're concerned, you can take off all the makeup as soon as we're finished photographing you."

"But I can't be the only one of your readers who can't afford makeup," Torey said. "So why glop it all over me?"

"I put hardly any on her," the makeup artist said. "Check it out, Jean."

"I believe you, Bernadette," Jean said, but she walked over to Torey anyway. "Torey, she really did leave you practically naked."

"My face must weigh a pound more than it did before," Torey said.

"Well, of course you have makeup on," Jean said. "And probably a little more than usual, because you'll need it for the camera. But you have beautiful skin and eyes, and all Bernadette has done is put a little eye shadow and foundation on. If you'll just look at yourself, you'll realize how beautiful you look."

"I look cheap," Torey muttered.

"Hardly," Ashley said, walking in with her hair wrapped in a towel turban. "You look sensational."

"It's the lipstick," Torey said, touching her lips with her tongue. "Do I have to have so much lipstick?"

"Yes," Jean said. "Now, keep quiet and behave yourself, Torey. Let Bernadette start working on one of the other girls."

"Me," Robin said, wanting to get it over with. Besides, there was always the chance Annie would be difficult too, and Bernadette might quit before she ever got to Robin.

"This one should be fun," Bernadette said, examining Robin's face carefully. "You have nice skin, you know that? Very clear."

112

"I wash it a lot," Robin said.

"Not with soap, I hope," Bernadette said. "Soap is poison for a face. Dries it out worse than the sun. Use a good facial cleanser."

"I will," Robin said, marveling that all those years of soap and water on her face hadn't completely destroyed her skin.

"This one is so cute and wholesome you just want to pinch her cheeks," Bernadette continued. "That the look you want for her, Jean?"

"That would be perfect," Jean said. "Not too young, though."

"Gotcha," Bernadette said. "Beige foundation," she announced as she started rubbing it into Robin's skin. "It's a good thing they work you too hard to get a suntan," she declared. "It's murder to work with a heavy tan. Especially for a winter issue."

Robin watched as best she could while Bernadette applied a rose-colored blush to her cheeks. In Bernadette's skillful hands, Robin's cheekbones became more noticeable, and her skin positively glowed.

"Eyes next," Bernadette said, and began tweezing Robin's eyebrows. The girls had all been instructed not to tweeze during their time at *Image*, so there was a lot that had to go. The tweezing smarted, the way it always did.

"You have nice eyebrows," Bernadette told her. "They just needed a little shaping."

Robin felt relieved.

"Violet eyeshadow," Bernadette announced, putting it on Robin's eyelids. "It'll bring out the blue in your eyes."

Robin had never realized her eyes had any blue in them. She'd always thought of them as dark. But if Bernadette saw blue, then maybe the camera would too. There was nothing wrong with that.

"Some nice navy liner," Bernadette continued. "And black mascara." She applied it gently. "There. Now, are you opposed to lipstick also?"

"No," Robin said. "Lipstick's fine with me."

"Excellent," Bernadette replied. "A nice light rose." She applied it with a brush and followed the contours of Robin's lips.

"There. That's it. The cheerleader of our dreams."

"Let me see," Jean said, and she and the editors walked over to check out Robin's new look. "Bernadette, you're a genius," she declared. "Robin, you look fabulous."

Robin stared at herself in the mirror. For one horrible moment, she knew exactly how Torey had felt. She had nothing against makeup, and wore it whenever she didn't oversleep in the morning, but with so much on, she felt like a painted woman. Still, she wasn't going to complain, not if Jean thought she looked fabulous.

Annie smiled at her. "You look great," she said. "Me next, I guess."

"Why don't you come with me, Robin," Donna Grey said. Robin followed the assistant fashion editor to the changing room.

"We wanted something casual for you," Donna declared. "Don't worry about your hair, Jason will comb it out again, but do be careful with your face when you put these on."

Robin wasn't quite sure how to be careful with her face, other than avoiding rubbing it against the cashmere sweater she was being handed. It was a soft aqua color, and it felt almost as good as her perfect silk blouse.

Donna gave her a pair of dark brown slacks and some aqua knee socks. "Let's see how all this looks," she said, so Robin tried them on for her.

"Perfect," Donna declared. "Jason is so good at what he does. You always were a pretty girl, but now you're something really special, Robin."

"Thank you," Robin said. "Should I wear shoes too?"

"Of course," Donna replied. "Classic loafers."

Robin slipped them on. The shoes at least felt familiar. She had a pair just like them at home.

"Let's see what Mrs. Brundege says," Donna said, and she and Robin started walking around the *Image* offices. Wherever they walked, people lined up to check her out. Robin felt like she was dressed in the emperor's new clothes.

"Very nice," she heard everyone say. "You look great, Robin.

Lovely, Donna. Just the right look."

Robin made a solemn vow that no matter what the temptation, she would never enter a beauty contest.

"Well, Mrs. Brundege," Donna said as they reached her office, "what do you think?"

Mrs. Brundege checked Robin over very carefully. "I think she's a wonder," she declared. "A girl with brains and beauty, and a fine talent for photography. We're lucky to have her as one of our interns."

"Thank you," Robin gasped. She hadn't been aware Mrs. Brundege knew she existed.

"So it's off to the studio?" Donna asked.

"Take her away," Mrs. Brundege replied.

Donna and Robin walked to the studio together. Even though Herb wouldn't be taking the pictures, Robin was sure she'd feel at home in the familiar environment.

But it was a strange sensation to be the model and not the photographer, she discoverd as soon as Jason was finished touching up her hair and she was positioned under the burning hot lights. They had just finished up with Torey, and once Robin's eyes adjusted to the light, she checked to see what Torey was wearing. No white gloves, she realized right away, and no circle pin either. But neither would have been inappropriate. Torey had on a very simple maroon wool dress and a dark gray blazer. She was wearing nylons and moderately high-heeled shoes, and she looked a minimum of twenty-two years old, and exceptionally gorgeous.

Robin didn't have a chance to be envious. The photographer started giving her detailed instructions on how she should pose, and Robin found herself pretending to be a model, smiling at a make-believe boyfriend, laughing at a nonexistent joke, thinking seriously about a philosophical comment nobody had made. She tilted her head one way and the next, turned to face right, then left, carried books, carried a camera, pretended to take a picture of the man who was taking pictures of her.

When she was finished, she walked over to talk with Torey, and Annie came in for her session. She was also in clothes that were appropriate for school, but her look was softer and prettier than either Torey's or Robin's. Annie had on an almost old-fashioned rose-colored dress with a ruffled round collar. The dress flared out slightly at the waist and went to just below her knees. She was also wearing nylons, and low pumps. Robin had never seen her cousin look so feminine.

"I feel like Alice in Wonderland," Annie declared. "This is not me at all."

"None of us are," Torey said. "We're all exaggerated versions of how they think we are."

"Can you imagine what Ashley's going to look like, then?" Robin asked.

None of them could. Robin contented herself with watching the photographer take his pictures of Annie. He went through the same routine with her as he had with Robin, but it was still interesting to see. Robin was no longer positive she wanted to be a fashion photographer, but she still was pleased to have another chance to see one at work.

Annie was finished for a full twenty minutes before there was any sign of Ashley. The rumors started way before that, though. They hated Ashley's haircut. Her makeup wasn't working. None of the clothes looked right. Mrs. Brundege had fired everybody. The makeover session was over. The whole idea of interns had been thrown out. *Image* had gone out of business.

When Ashley finally arrived, it was not an anticlimax. Her hair had been bobbed, short and quite severely, in a modern version of the Dutch-boy look. Her eyes had been made up to look twice their usual size, and her face, always thin, seemed gaunt. Her lips were now two bright red slashes.

She was wearing a red sweater dress that ended mid-thigh and was belted loosely at her hips. To complete the outfit, she had on black tights and high-heeled black shoes.

"It's the Paris tart look," Ashley declared as she posed under the lights. "Very big in Missouri this time of year."

"Do you really want to look like that?" Torey asked her.

"Sure," Ashley said. "Why not?"

Robin could think of several reasons, but she chose not to name them. If *Image* really was dressing them the way they thought the girls were, it seemed awfully unlikely Ashley was going to end up on the cover.

She turned out to be a great model, though, very relaxed and animated. The photographer had to work a lot less with her than he had with Robin or Annie, or, Robin suspected, Torey. Ashley gave him what he wanted. Robin got the feeling a few of the pictures would come out with Ashley looking like she was dressed up in her big sister's clothes, an innocent pretending to be sophisticated. Maybe those would be the ones used.

Finally the girls posed for some pictures together. At first it was tough to do, since it was hard to relax and act natural when they were being scrutinized so carefully by so many different people. But after a few minutes it almost felt normal, and the photographer started shooting more and more, and the editors were all smiling and nodding, and even Mrs. Brundege came in to congratulate them all.

When it was finally over, Robin was bone-tired, headachy, grouchy, itchy, and much to her surprise, still sick to her stomach. One makeover a lifetime, she decided, was more than enough.

13

"COME ON, ROBIN," Annie said. "You know it will be fun. Say yes."

Robin didn't know anything of the sort. In fact, the more she thought about it, the greater her doubts grew. "I don't know," she said. "Tim and I have so little time together."

"You have plenty of time together," Annie replied. "You must see him three or four times a week. And you always go out."

"Not always," Robin said defensively. The truth of the matter was, she and Tim guarded their time alone. There wasn't all that much time left to the summer, and they didn't care to share what little they had.

"It's just one night," Annie said. "And Tim and Harvey hit it off real well."

"But this sounds so weird," Robin said. "You want Tim and me and Ned and Torey to go out with you and Harvey and Ashley? That *is* what you're saying, isn't it?"

"Basically," Annie replied. "If Torey isn't even harder to convince than you are."

"Do you and Harvey and Ashley go out often?" Robin asked. "I didn't realize you liked Ashley that much."

"She was so nice about Harvey and me," Annie said. "I guess I feel I owe her one."

"But I thought she was dating Harvey also," Robin said. "Don't you think it's time you filled me in on your dirty little secret?"

"You're right," Annie said. "Everyone else knows, so you might as well. Harvey isn't going out with Ashley anymore. He hasn't since the night of the party. She's been going out with one of the guys in his band. A real sleazeball. Harvey hates him."

"What's his name?" Robin asked. "David Disaster?"

"He calls himself Morrison," Annie told her. "For Jim Morrison. Even Harvey doesn't know what his real name is. His hair is almost as long as mine, and he has tattoos on both arms, and he definitely is not premed. I don't know what Ashley sees in him, and neither does Harvey, who feels terribly responsible for it. He keeps making the four of us go out together so he can keep an eye out for trouble."

"That sounds like lots of fun," Robin said. "You enjoying your summer, Annie?"

"It's kind of interesting, actually," Annie said. "And Harvey really is sweet about it."

"Does Ashley have a date with this Morrison person on Saturday night?" Robin asked. "Are we all invited to protect her?"

"Morrison and Ashley don't make dates," Annie said. "He either shows or he doesn't. But this Saturday night we're all invited to see Infanticide perform at their club. That's really why I've asked you and Tim. I'm kind of nervous about going there with just Ashley. And I really want to see Harvey perform."

"I thought they didn't go on until late at night," Robin said.

"They don't," Annie replied. "But if all of us are going, there's a chance I can convince Jean to let us stay out an hour or two late just once. We'll all act as each other's chaperones."

"I still don't know," Robin told her. "It just doesn't seem like that great a way to spend an evening."

"Come on," Annie said. "Do I ever ask favors of you? And do I need to remind you that if it weren't for my grandmother, you wouldn't have met Tim in the first place?"

"That's not fair," Robin grumbled. "But all right. If you can convince Torey to go, and if Jean will let us, I'll get Tim. I've done almost everything else in New York. I might as well go to a punk-rock club."

"Oh, thank you!" Annie said, and gave her cousin a hug. "You'll have a great time, I promise."

Robin still had her doubts. But since she was sure Jean would never agree, it seemed a safe offer to make.

Jean, it turned out, was relatively easy to convince. Now that the girls had posed for the makeover article, she didn't care if they lost an hour or two of beauty sleep. And since Ned Brundege was going to be part of the party, the evening obviously had Mrs. Brundege's sanction.

Robin then set about convincing Torey, and she turned out to be fairly easy also. "I'm worried about Ashley," she said. "I want to see this Morrison person close up."

"You mean you'll actually let Ned spend money on you?" Robin asked.

Torey blushed. "He keeps trying to, whether I want him to or not," she replied. "At least this time it's for a good cause."

That left only Tim to convince. Robin waited until after they'd had dinner and were walking back to the hotel to bring it up.

"Do you know what those clubs are like?" Tim asked her.

Robin shook her head.

"They're noisy and smoky, and everybody drinks," he informed her. "Ned's the only one of us old enough to order drinks, so we'll be stuck sipping club soda all night long, and we won't be able to hear ourselves think, even before the bands start playing, and I hate cigarette smoke. It makes me sick to my stomach."

"It sounds like you don't like the idea," Robin said.

"You're right," Tim replied.

"We don't have to stay forever," Robin said. "But the only way Jean will let anybody go is if we all do. We can leave early."

"I don't understand why you're making such a big fuss about this," Tim said. "Do you want to go?"

"Not especially," Robin replied. "But it's important to Annie, and I want to do it for her."

"You always want to do things with them," Tim said. "Sometimes I feel like I'm not just dating you, I'm dating all of you."

"That's not fair," Robin said.

"That's how it feels, though," he said. "You never just talk about yourself. You certainly never just talk about me. It's always Annie this or Torey that or Ashley something else. You've made us go out on double dates twice now with Ned and Torey because you're worried that's the only way Torey will agree to go out with him. Do you know how many more Saturdays we have left, Robin?"

"No," Robin admitted.

"Three," he said. "Four if you can convince your parents to let you stay in New York the weekend after your internship is over. And then it's back to Ohio for you and Long Island for me."

"I don't want to think about that," Robin said.

"You may not want to, but it's the truth," Tim declared. "And I don't want to spend one of my last three Saturday nights with you someplace where I won't even be able to breathe."

"We'll do something else on Sunday," Robin suggested. "We'll jog in Central Park. We'll go swimming or horseback riding. Something wholesome and good for our lungs."

"I can't," Tim said. "My grandparents are coming into town on Sunday. I have to spend the day with them."

"I was counting on doing something with you Sunday," Robin said. "How long have you known about your grandparents?"

"For a couple of days now," he told her. "I'd really much rather spend the day with you, but my father won't let me. He says he's hardly seen me at all this summer, and my grandparents are coming in just for the day and I'd better plan to spend it with them if I know what's good for me."

"This is great," Robin said. They had reached the hotel, but she didn't feel like continuing their discussion in the lobby. "I have plans Saturday night and you have plans for Sunday. At least my plans included you."

"You mean you'd go to the club even without me?" Tim asked.

"Of course I will," Robin said. "If I don't, Annie can't. I have to go, just as much as you have to spend the day with your family."

"It's not the same thing at all," Tim said angrily.

"It sure is," Robin said. "Annie is my family. I'm spending the evening with my cousin. You're still welcome to come along if you want."

"You know perfectly well I don't want," Tim said. "I want to spend Saturday night alone with you."

"And I want to spend Sunday alone with you," Robin said. "I guess we don't always get what we want."

"I asked my father if I could bring you Sunday," Tim said. "He said no. He said my grandparents wanted to see me, not my girlfriend."

"My family is nicer," Robin said. "Annie told me to invite you."

"Annie's a real sweetheart, all right," Tim said.

"Don't you talk about my cousin that way!" Robin said.

"I'll talk about your stupid cousin any way I feel like," Tim shouted.

"And don't you call her stupid!" Robin shouted back.

"I'm going home," Tim said. "If you come to your senses, give me a call."

"I won't call you until you apologize," Robin informed him.

"I won't apologize," Tim said. "So I guess I'd better expect never to hear from you again."

"I guess so," Robin said. "I mean, I guess not." She was too angry to be sure what she meant.

"Well, it's been fun," Tim said. "See you on the cover." He turned his back on Robin and started walking away.

Robin stuck her tongue out at him, and then realized she was in the middle of New York City, where sophisticated people did not stand on street corners sticking their tongues out. The thought that she looked like a fool only made her madder. She'd go out Saturday night and have a great time without him. If he was unwilling to share his time with her friends, then he wasn't worth her time at all. Or something like that.

Robin wasn't sure about anything anymore except her anger and her confusion. Maybe some punk rock would clear her head.

She spent the next couple of days waiting for Tim to apologize, but he never did. The longer she went without hearing from him, the angrier she got. He had some nerve. He knew she didn't want to go to the dumb club, especially not without him. They only had three Saturday nights left. Why was he choosing to be so difficult about one of them?

She considered calling him, but her pride wouldn't let her. Besides, Annie was so grateful that she had agreed to go to the club that Robin knew she couldn't put herself in a position where she might get talked out of it. And as the time to go got closer and closer, her desire to go got weaker and weaker. By Saturday night it felt like she was preparing for an evening with the dentist.

"What do you wear to one of these places?" Robin asked Ashley as they dressed for the evening.

"Whatever you want," Ashley replied. "I'm going to wear this dress."

"It's so short," Robin said, watching Ashley slip it on. Even for Ashley, it showed a lot of leg.

"You can wear jeans if you want," Ashley said. "How about jeans and that blouse you bought way back?"

"Would that be okay?" Robin asked. "I won't be underdressed?"

"Nobody is going to care," Ashley said. "Nobody will even be able to see you. The lights at the club are real dim."

"How do you know?" Robin asked. "When have you been there?"

"Morrison's taken me a couple of times," Ashley said. "Of course, I've had to leave real early because of the curfew, but I still got some feel for the place. It's really fun, Robin. There are a lot of great-looking guys there. You won't miss Tim at all."

Robin knew that wasn't true. She missed him already. But Annie was depending on her, and she wasn't about to let her down.

Harvey had arranged to meet the girls at the club, so Ned got the job of picking the girls up at the hotel and taking them downtown. The four of them waited for him in the lobby, and sure enough, he showed up right on time.

Robin examined him carefully. He and Torey looked perfect together, tall, regal, and graceful. Although they held hands, Ned made a point of acting as all their escorts. He told Robin how sorry he was that Tim couldn't join them, and mentioned to Annie how much he was looking forward to hearing Harvey play. He even chatted pleasantly about Morrison with Ashley. His mother had obviously taught him well.

It was a fairly long cab ride downtown, and Robin wasn't thrilled with the neighborhood when she finally saw it. Still, there were plenty of people on the street, and a lot of them seemed to be going into the club.

Ned paid for the cab and escorted the girls inside. The place was so dark Robin could hardly see a thing. And Tim was right. It was thick with cigarette smoke. But Harvey met them almost immediately, and that made Robin feel better. Of course he was in full regalia for his performance that evening, but Annie didn't seem to mind. She and Harvey kissed hello, which only made Robin miss Tim even more.

"Is it always this crowded here?" Torey asked as Harvey showed them to their table.

"On weekends," he replied. "Infanticide is getting bigger and bigger. There's even a chance we might get a recording contract."

"Oh, Harvey, that would be great," Annie said.

"It wouldn't be a big company," Harvey said. "But sometimes these things lead to bigger clubs, better bookings. It might make paying for med school a little easier."

"I can't wait to hear you perform," Annie said. "I've been looking forward to this so much all week."

"And I've been looking forward to it too," Harvey said, giving Annie another kiss.

Robin found all this difficult to take. Her straight-arrow cousin, the one she always had to be better than, was kissing a guy with no eyebrows in the middle of a punk-rock club, surrounded by strangers in New York City. She only wished she'd brought her camera.

"I see you made it."

"Morrison," Ashley said.

Robin squinted. Her eyes had begun to tear from all the smoke, but she was determined to see what this character looked like.

Annie had gotten the hair and the tattoos right, but she'd left out the very real scar running down the left side of his face, and the meanness in his eyes, and the missing front tooth. Harvey Horrible looked fragile in comparison.

"This is Morrison," Ashley announced. "Morrison, this is everybody else."

"I see," he said. He ran his fingers up and down Ashley's arm. "Wanna split?" he asked her. "I don't have to be back here for another couple of hours. Right, Harv?"

"An hour," Harvey said. "At most an hour. Why don't you just stay here with us, Morrison? You don't want to be late."

"I'm willing to take the chance," Morrison declared. "Come on, Ashley. You can join your buddies later."

"All right," Ashley said, and got up. Morrison half-pushed her away from the table, but Robin didn't notice Ashley resisting.

"So that's Morrison," Torey said. "Is he as bad as he looks, Harvey?"

"Probably." Harvey grimaced. "He doesn't hang around much with the group. He's a good guitarist, though, and we can't afford to get rid of him."

"He gives me the willies," Annie said, and snuggled up to Harvey.

"I'm sure Ashley can take care of herself," Ned declared, putting his arm around Torey.

Robin stared at the two couples and felt very incomplete. She didn't miss Tim all that much when she was working, although she certainly did think of him on occasion. But watching Torey and Annie couple off made her feel alone and unhappy.

It wasn't that late yet. And she'd done what she had to do, made it possible for Annie to get a chance to hear Harvey play. There was nothing keeping her from leaving the club, going back to the hotel, and seeing if Tim was home to be apologized to.

"I have an awful headache," she half-lied to Torey and Annie. "Harvey, would you be offended if I didn't stay to hear you play?"

"No," he said. "Morrison gives me a headache too sometimes. But how will you get home?"

"I'll take a cab," Robin said. "I'll be okay once I get there."

"I'll go out with you while you hail one," Harvey said. "It shouldn't take too long."

"Are you sure you're all right?" Annie asked her. "Do you want me to go back with you?"

"Absolutely not," Robin said. "Enjoy your late night out. Have a good time. I'll expect all the details in the morning."

She and Harvey made their way out of the club together. Hailing a cab turned out to be quite easy, since a lot of people came to the club by taxi. Robin tapped her foot impatiently the entire trip home. She had to talk to Tim. She had to make it up with him. She had to see him on their third-from-last Saturday together.

She ran up to her hotel room, after first checking in, and called Tim immediately. There was no answer.

Robin stared at the walls of her hotel room. It was Saturday night and she was in New York City, and somehow she had managed to arrange to spend it all alone with nothing to do and nobody to do it with. She could have spent it with Tim, having a good time. She could have spent it with her friends, having an interesting time. But somehow she'd managed to arrange it so she was all alone, having a miserable time.

She spent the evening calling Tim every half-hour on the half-hour, waiting for him to answer. He never did. Between calls she tried to watch TV, attempted to read a book, started a letter to her best friend at home. She showered and washed her hair to get the smell of the club off her body. She polished her fingernails. She did some exercises. She hand-washed some lingerie. She went to the deli and bought a box of chocolate-chip cookies, all of which she ate. And she called Tim and let the phone ring eight times at first, then ten, and finally twelve.

She gave up trying to reach him at eleven, by which time she was so angry at him for not being home, she'd forgotten all about being bored. He probably had a date with some beautiful New York City girl. He'd probably picked the fight with her just so he could break it off, so he could date this beautiful New York City girl. He didn't have plans with his grandparents. He probably didn't even have grandparents. He probably had a date scheduled with a different beautiful New York City girl for every day of the week.

She'd show him, Robin decided as she tossed and turned her way to sleep. She'd go back to Ohio and forget all about him. She'd date all the boys in Elmsford. No, she'd date all the boys in Ohio. If she had to, she'd date all the boys in the entire Midwest.

And Tim wouldn't be able to forget her, because she'd be picked to be on the cover of *Image*. Wherever he'd go her face would follow him. He'd be haunted, and she'd be having the time of her life.

Robin shut her eyes even tighter. She didn't need Tim. She didn't need anybody. She was Robin Louise Schyler and she could make it on her own.

14

ROBIN KNEW SHE should have been more excited about being on television for the first time, but nothing was much fun since her quarrel with Tim. The other girls seemed to be excited enough. Annie had gotten her hair restyled, since she hadn't bothered maintaining it after the makeover. Ashley had spent a half-hour putting together a decent outfit for Torey, and Torey hadn't even objected this time, since her family would be able to watch her on TV when the show was aired. But none of them had been able to talk Robin into having a good time."

"I know it's only cable," Annie said. "But it's national cable. We get this station in our system."

"We get it in ours too," Robin said. It was a station devoted to shows for kids and teenagers. Robin had watched it on occasion herself.

"So your parents will be able to watch you," Annie said. "As well as my parents. And all your friends will see you. You'll be a star."

"Besides, everybody will get to see Torey and me," Ashley pointed out. "Just think how much time that will save you when people ask what we were like."

"My family will see you too," Torey said. "And I want them to see you smiling and happy. You're prettier that way."

"Face it, Robin," Ashley said. "You're extremely boring when you're unhappy."

"I suppose you're fascinating when you're unhappy," Robin said, wishing they would all shut up.

"I certainly am," Ashley replied. "I'm given to big dramatic gestures. You just get sulky."

"Nobody's telling you not to make up with Tim," Annie said. "The two of you had your fight almost a week ago. That's just the right amount of time to call him and make up."

"I tried calling him," Robin said. "What do you think I was doing Saturday night? He never answered the phone, so why should I be the one to keep trying? Let him call me."

Annie shrugged her shoulders. "If you feel that way, fine," she said. "But stop moping around. Be so gorgeous on TV that every boy in America will want you. Except for Harvey."

"Harvey isn't exactly my type," Robin told her. "I prefer natural eyebrows."

"He's growing them back," Annie said defensively. "You know, Ashley, you're right. Robin has gotten sulky and obnoxious."

"She never said 'obnoxious,' " Robin said.

"I would have eventually," Ashley said.

The phone rang in Robin and Ashley's room. Ashley answered. "It's Jean," she told the other girls. "Time for us to go."

The girls took the elevator downstairs in relative silence, then met Jean in the lobby. They piled into a cab and went to Eleventh Avenue, where the studio was located. Robin scolded herself the entire trip over. The girls were right. She had been grouchy and obnoxious all week long. She didn't have that much time left in New York, and all she was doing was ruining it for herself, if not for everybody else. Either she and Tim would make up, or they wouldn't. Either way, she'd live.

"Welcome, girls," Carla Everest, the show's producer, said as they walked into the studio. "Hi Jean. I'm glad you could all make it."

"Thanks for having us," Jean said. "Do we have time for a quick tour?"

"Absolutely," Carla replied. "And I want you to meet Don Myers. He's the star of the show. Don, come on over here."

A handsome man walked over. He was dressed informally in shirt and slacks, and he'd loosened his tie. "Hi, girls," he said. "I'm looking forward to talking with all of you."

"Hello," the girls said. Robin wondered if the others felt as shy as she did.

"It'll be a real help if I know which one of you is which," Don said. "Which one of you is Ashley Boone?"

Ashley raised her hand.

Don went through the same process with all of the other girls. He stared at each one as though to commit them to memory. Then he flashed them a big smile, assured them they'd all have a wonderful time on the show, and wandered away to put on his makeup and change into his official TV clothes.

Carla showed them the green room, which was where the girls would wait until they were introduced on the show, and the studio where the show would be shot. There were bleachers for the audience that looked like they would hold about eighty people. Robin knew from seeing the show in the past that the audience would be filled with teenagers, who would have a chance to ask questions later in the day. Carla showed the girls where they would be sitting; the stage was set up to resemble a living room, and two of the girls would be on one side of Don, and two on the other. Then the girls were whisked off to the makeup room, where each one of them took her turn. This time Torey didn't complain about feeling painted, even though the makeup that was put on her was even heavier than the stuff used in the makeovers.

They didn't have to wait long in the green room, but it seemed endless to Robin. She could hear the audience pile onto the bleacher benches, and she wished she were one of them. Her stomach hurt, and she entertained herself by thinking of the thousand different ways she could make a fool of herself on television.

"Just remember, girls, you're representing *Image*," Jean said, and smiled briskly at them. Robin felt the urge to punch her teeth out.

"You mean we can't spit or curse or take our clothes off?" Ashley asked. Annie tittered.

"That's exactly what I mean," Jean said, continuing to smile. "Make us proud of you, Ashley."

"Yes, ma'am," Ashley drawled.

"Time, girls," Carla said, sticking her head in. "Torey, why don't you go first, and then you, Robin, and now Ashley and Annie."

The girls followed her instructions and left the green room, walking directly onto the stage. Eighty strange teenagers applauded their entrance.

The lights were very bright, and Robin tried hard not to blink or squint. She sat down between Torey and Don, and turned to face Don. She also checked to see where the cameras were located. The one with the red light on was the one in use, she knew, from the preshow coaching Jean had given them the day before. They were to make eye contact naturally, with whomever they were talking to, but it never hurt to be aware which of the two cameras was in use.

Don introduced each of the girls to the audience, giving their names, where they were from, and what their particular internship was. He then turned to Annie and asked her how the summer was going.

Annie answered calmly and naturally. Under Don's questioning she described what her job entailed.

"And how about you, Robin?" Don asked. "How did you get the internship with *Image*?"

Robin was so startled that he'd picked on her to ask, that she didn't have a chance to get tongue-tied. "I sent in some photographs I'd taken," she told him. "And I filled out a thousand forms and wrote an essay."

"But it was your photographs that finally convinced them that you should be the photography intern," Don said.

Robin thought for a moment about her demographics. "It wasn't just that," she said. "There are a lot of awfully talented photographers out there, and it's possible some of the other girls sent in pictures that were better than mine. It was a combination of things."

"Like what?" Don persisted.

"I had to write an essay on what I hoped to gain from the internship," Robin said, choosing her words carefully. "Obviously, if I thought I was the world's most gifted photographer, I wouldn't be open to learning from the professionals I'd be working with. And I had to get letters of recommendation from people to prove I was capable of hard work. Believe me, they work you hard at *Image*. And I had to send them a picture of myself. I don't think they really cared if I was Miss America or not, but they didn't want anybody with two heads."

"How do you feel about that, Ashley?" Don asked, turning his attention away from Robin. "Do you feel your looks had something to do with your getting the internship?"

"I don't think it's a coincidence that we're all very pretty," Ashley replied. "One of us is going to be on the cover, after all. You never see ugly girls on the cover of *Image*."

"That's an interesting point," Don said. "Torey, do you think *Image* is too appearance-oriented? Do you feel you're being judged as much on your looks as your talent?"

"I've always been judged on my looks," Torey said. "People have always been just a little nicer to me because they think I'm pretty. I don't know why *Image* should be different."

"I think *Image* is too appearance-conscious," Annie said. "I was told to go on a diet practically the moment I arrived in New York. And I was very carefully watched to make sure I stayed on it and lost the amount of weight they wanted."

"But it's a fashion magazine," Ashley said. "Of course they wanted pretty girls. Of course they wanted us to be as pretty as we could be. Half the magazine is devoted to fashion and appearance. They don't care what the I.Q. of their models is, just as long as they photograph well."

"I agree with Annie," Robin said. "I buy *Image*, and while I enjoy the fashion spreads, I read the magazine for the articles and fiction. And I think most of my friends read it for the same reasons."

"I read it for the fashion," Ashley said. "Come on, now, Robin. How many of those articles really pertain to your own life? How to get a boy to ask you out? What to do if your parents are splitting up? How to handle your first job interview? Is going steady really for you? Be serious."

"Do you find the articles pertain to your life, Torey?" Don asked, clearly enjoying the discussion going on.

"Some more than others," Torey replied. "Which I assume would be true of any magazine."

"All right," Don said. "You in the audience. Let's have a show of hands. How many of you read *Image* on a regular basis?"

About half the kids raised their hands.

"And how many of you read it for the fashion spreads?" Don continued.

Roughly half of the hands remained up.

"And articles?"

The other half came up.

"So it seems to be a fifty-fifty split," Don said. "Which is probably just the way the *Image* editorial staff wants it. Annie, knowing that, if you were editor-in-chief of *Image*, what changes would you make?"

"I'd still cut the fashion section in half," Annie said. "And I'd certainly change their approach on food."

"I agree," Robin said. "I mean, their food articles are really cute, but they're useless. We just did a spread on zucchini cupcakes. I'm sure they're delicious, but I'm not sure anyone's ever going to make them. My mother and father both work, and a lot of the time I'm in charge of making supper. There are lots of teenagers in that position, and we don't need recipes for zucchini cupcakes. We need main-course recipes that are easy to make."

There was an actual smattering of applause.

"We could use articles on grocery shopping, too," Torey said. "Kids nowadays have a lot of responsibilities around the house. And they have part-time jobs too. They could use articles on how to handle jobs, and taxes, and savings."

"I'm sure these are all things *Image* will start thinking about,"

Don said. "Do you girls feel you've had a significant input at the magazine? Do the editors listen to your opinions?"

"I know they listen to me," Ashley said. "Of course, all I do is lowly fashion, which nobody here seems to think is worth anything, but ideas I've suggested have been used."

"Oh, Ashley," Torey said. "Nobody says the fashion articles aren't important."

"Sometimes I think you all feel that way," Ashley said.

"I don't," Robin said. "I love looking at the pictures of the models and seeing what clothes are fashionable. I've gotten ideas for outfits from *Image* for years now. I just wouldn't buy it for the clothes alone."

"Speaking of *Image*'s editorial staff, we have one of them here," Don said. "Jean Kingman, who is in charge of the summer internship program, came with the girls today. She's been waiting offstage to make an important announcement."

Robin shot Annie a look. Annie shrugged her shoulders almost imperceptibly.

Jean walked out, carrying an artist's portfolio. The audience applauded her, while Ashley and Annie moved over to make room for her.

"Jean, have you been listening to all the ideas the girls have been suggesting?" Don asked her.

"I certainly have," Jean said. "And I want to make it very clear that the interns do have an influence on our future editorial policies. That's a major reason why we have the internships every year. *Image* pays a lot of attention to the letters its readers send in, but we find it very helpful to have our readership represented in person for eight weeks. For example, Robin and Torey's comments about the food articles just now were very well taken. I intend to discuss them at our next major editorial meeting."

"That's great, Jean," Don said. "Now, I know you have a surprise for us. Do you care to tell us what is in that portfolio you're carrying?"

"I'd be delighted, Don," Jean said. "As Ashley mentioned earlier, one of these four girls is going to be on the cover of *Image* in six months. We have a special issue devoted each year to our interns, and one of the four girls is always picked to be the cover girl for that issue."

"That must be a great honor," Don declared.

"It certainly is," Jean said. "We wait until the girls have completed their makeovers and are photographed professionally before the final decision is made. Looks are not the only criterion used to make our choice. We feel the intern that best represents what *Image* stands for is the one who should be on the cover."

"It must be a very difficult choice," Don said.

"This year it was unusually so," Jean said. "Each of our interns is so special this year, we considered having all four of them on the cover. But finally we decided to stick with tradition and pick one intern to represent them all."

"And you're here today to tell us which lucky girl that will be," Don said.

"I am," Jean said with her standard smile. She began unzipping her portfolio. "I've brought with me the photograph we'll be using. Naturally, the layout of the cover will be slightly different, but I thought you might like to see what the picture on the cover will be."

"Of course we're interested," Don said. "I bet the four girls on this stage are very interested indeed."

"I do want everyone to understand that making this choice was very hard," Jean said. "Our meeting lasted several hours, with each of the girls being proposed by several different editors as being the perfect choice. But finally, consensus was reached."

Let it be me, Robin prayed. Let her take out my picture.

"And this is the photograph that finally decided us," Jean announced, removing the photograph and displaying it to the audience.

For a moment Robin tried twisting to see what the picture was. But then she noticed Annie was looking at the monitor, so she looked there as well.

It was Torey. It was a Torey so breathtakingly beautiful Robin almost didn't recognize her. But still, it was Torey.

"Well, Torey Jones," Don said. "How do you feel about finding out you're going to be an *Image* cover girl?"

"That's really me?" Torey asked. "I look that good?"

Don laughed. "How do all of you in the audience feel about the choice?" he asked. "I don't want this to turn into a beauty contest, but I would appreciate some honest opinions. Yes . . . you, young man in the fourth row. You have an opinion?"

"I can't really be objective," a very familiar boy's voice said. "They all seem to be very fine girls. But I think they should have picked someone who looks a little less like a fashion model. Someone like Robin."

"Tim?" Robin squeaked.

"You know this boy?" Don asked her.

"I guess I do," Robin said, her heart singing. "We've been dating all summer."

"You, Tim," Don said. "What's it been like, dating an *Image* intern?"

"It's been wonderful," Tim said. "But I guess it depends on which intern you date."

The audience laughed. Robin managed to laugh along with them.

The next ten minutes of the show were agony for Robin. But eventually the show was over and the girls were thanked and sent to the makeup room to have their faces cold-creamed back to normal.

Tim met them outside. He walked right over to Robin and hugged her. Robin loved the feeling of being in his arms.

"How did you know I would be here?" Robin asked.

"Ned told me," Tim said. "He knew they'd be announcing the cover girl, and I figured I wanted to be here to celebrate or commiserate, whichever was appropriate."

"I tried calling you all Saturday night," Robin said.

"My grandparents came in a day early," Tim told her. "We went out to dinner and then the theater. And then I would have called you except I figured you'd want to kill me and you deserved to, and I wanted to see you in person, but I got shy all of a sudden.

I don't know. Do you forgive me?"

"Only if you forgive me," Robin said.

They hugged again, and then they kissed. Robin didn't care who saw them. She never wanted to leave Tim's embrace again.

"I don't believe it," Ashley said, walking over to them. "Hi, Tim. Do you believe it?"

"What?" Tim asked, breaking away reluctantly from Robin.

"They picked Torey," Ashley said.

"Oh, that's right," Robin said. "You picked Annie."

"I thought they'd pick me," Ashley said sharply. "They should have picked me. The only reason they didn't was that I was too sharp for them. They wanted a hick, not somebody with sophistication. I'm better-looking than Torey. I have so much more style. They should have picked me."

"I know how you feel, Ashley," Robin said. "I was disappointed too. But Torey is beautiful, and she looked great in that photograph. She was a perfectly reasonable choice."

"They should have picked me," Ashley muttered, and started walking away from them.

"Ashley, where are you going?" Robin asked.

"To find Morrison," Ashley replied. "And forget my sorrows."

Robin thought about trying to stop Ashley, but realized there was no point. Ashley would calm down. Besides, she had only two more Wednesdays left in New York, and this was one she intended to spend with Tim.

15

FRIDAY MORNING, ROBIN was hanging out at the studio, waiting for Herb to return from the darkroom, when the telephone rang. It startled her. She'd been thinking about how there was only one more week left, and one and a half weekends. It turned out there was a farewell party scheduled for the girls a week from Saturday, so she'd made her plane reservations for Sunday instead.

Nine days wasn't a heck of a lot of time, she was thinking when she heard the phone. She picked it up with a sigh.

"Robin? This is Shelley."

"Sure, Shelley," Robin said. "What's up?"

"I just got a message for you to go to Mrs. Brundege's office," Shelley told her.

"Okay," Robin said. "Do you know what it's about?"

"Not really," Shelley said. "I was told to find you and send you over immediately. So I'd get a move on."

"I'm on my way," Robin said, and hung up. She left a note for Herb telling him where she was going, and started the walk through the corridors. She had the uncomfortable feeling of having been summoned to the principal's office. Still, she couldn't remember having done anything wrong recently, so she was probably safe. Nonetheless, she wouldn't have minded seeing a friendly face as she made her way.

She opened the door, and Mrs. Brundege's secretary didn't even say hello. She just picked up the phone and said, "Robin Schyler is here."

Something about the way last name sounded scared Robin. She searched her brain frantically to see what she could possibly have done. But nothing came to mind.

"Go on in," Mrs. Brundege's secretary said to her. "She's expecting you."

Robin assumed she was, since she had summoned her in the first place. She opened the door to Mrs. Brundege's office and found her and Jean sitting behind the desk. The situation was becoming less and less appealing.

"Sit down, Robin," Mrs. Brundege said, so Robin did. For the life of her, she couldn't think of anything bad she'd done. Was this possibly *Image*'s way of announcing good news? But that, she knew, was wishful thinking.

"We have a very serious problem," Mrs. Brundege told her. "And we have reason to believe you are in some way involved."

Robin choked down a request for a lawyer. What was going on?

"Does this look familiar to you?" Mrs. Brundege asked, and handed Robin a sheet of paper.

Robin stared at it. It was a black-and-white duplicate, crudely printed, of the cover of the intern issue of *Image*. She recognized it from the TV show. Only where Torey's picture should have been was one of Ashley instead, wearing the exact same outfit Torey had had on.

Robin looked at it for a full minute before handing it back to Mrs. Brundege. If she'd been confused before, that was nothing compared with how she felt now. "What is that?" she finally asked.

"Are you saying you've never seen it before?" Jean asked.

"Yes," Robin said, starting to get mad. "I have never seen it before. I don't even know what it is. What's going on?"

"As I'm sure you can see, it's a duplicate of one of our future

covers," Mrs. Brundege said. "It was left on my desk this morning.
The only way the cover could have been duplicated was if somebody had taken the board dummy from the art department, substituted Ashley's picture for Torey's, and then returned it. We
checked the records, and you're listed as having signed the dummy
out and returned it."

"Let me see that," Robin said, so Mrs. Brundege gave her
the sheet. "That isn't my signature," Robin said when she located
her name. "That isn't even a forgery of my signature. It's just my
name."

"So you swear you have nothing to do with this?" Mrs. Brundege asked. "I hope you realize the seriousness of the situation."

Robin didn't completely, but she knew it was a relief not to
be guilty. "I had nothing to do with this," she declared.

The phone rang before Mrs. Brundege had a chance to re-
spond. She picked it up, listened for a moment, and then said,
"Send her in." A few seconds later, Ashley entered the room. She
seemed startled to see Robin there. Robin felt considerably less
startled.

"Sit down, Ashley," Mrs. Brundege said, so Ashley took the
chair next to Robin's. "We were wondering if you could tell us
anything about this?" And she showed Ashley the mock cover.

"Do you like it?" Ashley asked, and Robin was shocked to
hear the hope in her voice.

"Are you admitting, then, that you had something to do with
it?" Jean asked.

Robin yearned to warn Ashley to keep her mouth shut, but
she knew it wouldn't do any good.

"I had everything to do with it," Ashely said. "I knew you
hadn't really considered my picture for the cover because of that
outfit they'd put me in—you know Mrs. Brundege, the magazine
editors—and I thought that if you only had a chance to see me in
something decent, something more *Image*, if you know what I
mean, you'd reconsider. Torey may be more classically beautiful
than me, but I look a lot more like a model. So I reconstructed
the outfit and got my picture taken. See. I have glossies of me in

the outfit, if you want to see them." She paused for a moment, dug through her oversized bag, and handed pictures to Mrs. Brundege and Jean. They stared at the pictures for what felt like an eternity, and then put them back down on the desk.

"I think they came out really well," Ashley said. "Don't you? Anyway, I figured the best possible presentation would be in the form of an *Image* cover, so I borrowed one and used it. The copy didn't come out nearly as well as I'd hoped, but I figured if you were interested, I could show you the glossy. What do you think?"

"How did you get the dummy?" Mrs. Brundege asked.

"I signed out for it," Ashley said.

"Using your own name?" Mrs. Brundege persisted.

Ashley paused for a moment, and drew back almost imperceptibly. "Why are you asking?" she finally said.

"We couldn't find your name on the sign-out sheet," Mrs. Brundege told her.

"I used Robin's," Ashley said. "Sorry, Robin, but I figured nobody would think twice if they saw your name. You work in the art department, after all. It never occurred to me Robin might get into trouble over it."

"Robin isn't in trouble," Mrs. Brundege said, but Robin no longer felt any relief over the announcement. "Who took the picture for you, Ashley?"

"Jessie King," Ashley said. "I wanted the best, you know, so I called her up, and I told her Robin suggested I contact her. It was no problem for me to find her phone number, since Robin had left her card on her bureau drawer. Oh, maybe you don't know. Robin and I have been sharing a room all summer long. It was supposed to be Robin and Annie, you know, but they're cousins, you know, and they decided they didn't want to share a room. I'm sure you know all that by now, don't you?"

"Now we do," Jean said. Robin didn't know whether to cry or to kill.

"That's not the issue here," Mrs. Brundege said. "You paid Jessie King to take the picture?"

"And lots more," Ashley said. "I paid her to shoot a portfolio's

141

worth. Only I figured the rest of the pictures could wait until this weekend. The only one there was a rush on was the one for the mock cover. I think it turned out really well. Of course, that outfit isn't exactly my style, but I wanted to make a point. And for that, I think it's very effective."

"How did you intend to pay Ms. King?" Mrs. Brundege asked.

"Oh, I have the money," Ashley said. "My mother is always sending me stacks of the stuff. I don't even have to ask for it; she just ships it to me. She sends me my allowance, and then she gets a little drunk and can't remember whether she sent it to me, so she sends it to me again. And then she feels guilty that she should forget something that important, so she sends me more. I've been getting my allowance three or four times a week all summer. Plus my salary, of course. So I've had plenty of money, and I figured I might as well spend it on something important, something that could affect my entire future. An investment, you might say."

"I don't believe you," Robin said, finally exploding. "You used my name, and you forged my signature, and you went through my stuff, and you ratted on me right now, and you don't even care?"

"I didn't forge your name," Ashley said. "I just signed it. A forgery is when you make it look like the real thing. I don't know how to do that. And I didn't tell Jessie I was you. I just used your name. People do that all the time." She smiled at Robin.

"Do you need me for anything else?" Robin asked Mrs. Brundege.

"No," Mrs. Brundege said. "And I'm sorry to have involved you in this situation."

"That's all right," Robin said. "That wasn't your fault."

"Thank you, Robin," Mrs. Brundege said. "I'm sure we'll be talking with you later about your rooming situation."

"All right," Robin said. She'd worry about that when she had to. In the meantime, it was enough to get away from the atmosphere in that office. She didn't know what was going to happen to Ashley, but she felt nothing but relief that it wasn't going to happen to her.

It drove her half-crazy, but she waited the half-hour until lunch to locate Torey and Annie to tell them what had happened. She found she was shaking as she related the story in the relative privacy of a booth in the building's coffee shop.

"I don't believe Ashley did all that," Annie said. "What an idiot she is."

"And mean," Robin said. "I just can't get over how she involved me. I thought we were friends."

"It wasn't just you," Annie said. "What she did to Torey was rotten to."

"What did she do to me?" Torey asked.

"She tried to get you off the cover," Annie said. "Of course we've all been jealous that you ended up on the cover. You think I lost all that weight without hoping for the payoff? But they picked you, understandably, and that was that. It hurts, but you don't lose any sleep over it. Well, no more than a night's worth. You sure don't go out and try to convince Mrs. Brundege to take you off the cover and put somebody else on."

"I hate that cover," Torey said. "I really hate it. This summer I made friends of my own, friends who didn't have to be involved with my family situation, and that meant so much to me. It's insane to think something as meaningless as the cover should get between us. I thought the four of us were something special."

"Do you mean to tell me you're not angry at Ashley?" Robin asked. "I sure am."

"I'm mad at *Image* for promising the four of us something only one of us can have," Torey said. "The only thing I feel for Ashley is pity."

"Sometimes your nobility drives me crazy," Annie declared. "Don't you have any baser instincts, Torey?"

"Of course not," Torey replied. "I can't afford them."

In spite of herself, Robin joined in the laughter.

"Did you see Ashley after you left the office?" Annie asked Robin.

Robin shook her head. "For all I know, she's still being grilled by Mrs. Brundege."

"More likely she's back at the hotel," Torey said. "All alone, and scared silly. I'm going to go there and see how she is."

"I'll go," Robin said. "She might not even want you to know what she did. If Mrs. Brundege just chewed her out, she may hope nobody else will hear about it."

"Good point," Torey said. "Okay, you go over. I'll tell Shelley where you are if you don't get back to the office for a while."

"Thanks," Robin said, and left some money for the check. Not that she'd have a chance to eat more than a mouthful. As soon as she realized it would be a while before she'd have a chance to eat again, her appetite returned full force. It was clearly destined to be one of those days.

She walked back to the hotel, stopping on the way to buy a pretzel from a vendor, and munched on it thoughtfully as she walked. Ashley had found herself in a bad jam and had tried to pull down everybody else with her. Not, perhaps, the way Robin would have handled the situation, but then again, she wasn't Ashley, thank goodness. Although she wouldn't mind getting three or four allowances a week.

She went straight up to her room, and heard noises in there. Torey had been right. She really did understand Ashley in a way Robin never would.

She unlocked the door without giving Ashley any warning. It was hard to tell who was more shocked, Ashley at the sight of Robin, or Robin at what she was seeing.

Strewn over both beds were all of Ashley's clothes. Her suitcases were on the floor, half-filled with clothes thrown in them.

"What's going on?" Robin asked.

"What does it look like?" Ashley asked. "I've been kicked out. What are you doing here?"

"I don't know," Robin said. "I mean, I just figured I'd see how you were. They kicked you out?"

"Did they ever," Ashley said, going to the closet and yanking out another pile of blouses. "It seems what I did wasn't just a sin. It was a flat-out crime. They could have me arrested for theft or embezzlement or something if they really wanted to. I'm getting off lucky that they're just sending me home early. They're not even going to kick me out of the issue. Generous of them, isn't it?" She began ripping the blouses off their hangers.

"I don't understand," Robin said. "What kind of crime?"

"Mrs. Brundege explained it to me," Ashley said, tossing the blouses onto the floor. "You're not allowed to take unpublished issues of *Image* out of the office. What if the competition got to see them? What if you were selling them to the competition? What if you took the *Image* logo and put a pornographic picture on the cover? Great idea. I only wish I'd thought of it."

"And for that they're kicking you out?" Robin asked. She cleared off a space on her bed to sit down.

"If I had just substituted my picture for Torey's, or just left the picture on Mrs. Brundege's desk, then they'd be angry, but they wouldn't send me home early," Ashley said, sitting on the floor, surrounded by blouses. "I'd be a bad sport, which is a sin but not a crime. But just because I borrowed their precious board dummy for a few hours, then it's prison time. But they decided to be generous and just send me home a few days early. That's what she said. A few days early. It's nine full days, and they're sending me back to a prison worse than any they could find for me in New York."

"Don't exaggerate," Robin said. "Sure, your mother will be mad, but she'll get over it."

"You don't understand," Ashley said, and started removing the blouses from their hangers again. "It isn't my mother. She won't care. It's the old man. My grandfather. He's going to be furious at me."

"I'm sure when you explain it to him . . ." Robin said, feeling extremely uncomfortable.

"He's going to be furious," Ashley said. "Not at what I did. That he might even admire. But that I handled it so badly. That I got caught and punished. He's going to get so angry. And what's worse, he's going to be satisfied, too. He's always so sure I'm going to mess up, it makes him happy when I live up to his expectations."

Robin didn't know what to say. So she began folding the

145

clothes on her bed.

"I see you're glad to be rid of me too," Ashley said. "Well, I can't say I blame you. I shouldn't have used your name, and I know I shouldn't have told them you'd switched rooms. I really am sorry about that. Do you believe me?"

"I do," Robin said, but she couldn't make eye contact. She didn't want to have to look at the pain and desperation in Ashley's eyes.

"Mrs. Brundege said she'd call home to tell them I'd be arriving tomorrow," Ashley continued. "I guess she didn't trust me to make the call. Which was smart of her. She had Jean make the reservations for me, while I sat there. Jean is supposed to take me to the airport tomorrow. Lucky Jean."

"That's part of her job," Robin said.

"Jean hates my guts," Ashley said. "Oh, well. Why should she be different from anybody else?"

"Oh, come on, now," Robin said. "Everybody doesn't hate you, Ashley. You broke the rules and you got caught and you're being punished. That happens to everybody at some point or other. And your family will be mad, and then they'll get over it, and the school year will start, and your mother will keep giving you tons of money, and you can relax and have a good time."

"You really don't understand," Ashley said. "Well, why should you? It's not your family. Your family is the American ideal, all loving and happy."

"We've had our share of pain," Robin said. "More than our share, actually."

"Oh, sure, the tragedy of Caro, your beloved sister," Ashley said. "I bet you were happy when she died. Oh, not on the surface. Maybe you didn't even realize it for a while. But inside, you were happy. You lost your competition. Now you'd be number one automatically. You must have loved that."

"I hate you," Robin shouted. "You're cruel and selfish, and I hate you. Why haven't you left already? What's keeping you here, anyway?"

"Nothing," Ashley said, getting up. She stepped on her

blouses as she walked toward the door. "You're absolutely right, Robin. Nothing is keeping me here anymore. Good-bye, Robin. See you around." She grabbed her bag, opened the door, and left the room.

"Shut up," Robin muttered.

"Don't worry," Ashley said. "I already have." She grabbed her bag, opened the door and left the room.

Robin stared at her bed, with Ashley's clothes half-folded on it. She started throwing them off her bed, one by one, but then by the handful, wishing they would break as they fell, instead of just dropping gently onto the floor. She needed to hear something breaking, needed to know she had succeeded in destroying something. She got off the bed and walked over to Ashley's bureau, taking no care about what she stepped on.

All she could find there worth breaking was Ashley's travel clock. It wasn't much, but it would have to do. Robin picked it up and threw it across the room. It took three throws before it finally cracked, and once it did, Robin didn't feel any better at all.

She picked up the clock, put it back on the bureau, and sat down again on her bed. It was just a matter of time, she knew, before the anger gave way to guilt. It was even possible the guilt would turn into concern before too long.

Robin stared at the mess in her room, and compared it to the mess she'd made with Ashley. Roughly comparable, she decided, and she buried her head in her pillow so she wouldn't have to deal with either.

16

AT THE TIME, she thought she was awake when the telephone rang, but later, when she had a chance to think about what had happened, she remembered her first thought at the sound had been: "It's about Caro." She got to the phone on the second ring, though, and sounded awake, at least to her own ears, when she said hello.

"It's me," Ashley whimpered.

"Where are you?" Robin asked. According to Ashley's travel clock, it was three A.M., but it was impossible to know if it was still telling accurate time.

"I'm in a phone booth," Ashley said, half-crying. "Robin, I'm hurting so much."

"Take a breath and tell me what happened," Robin instructed her. She was fully awake now, and flooded with fear.

"I took Morrison's motorcycle," Ashley said, sounding a little better. "And I've been riding and riding and I lost control and I hit a telephone pole, I think, something tall, and I flew off, and I've been trying to walk, but it hurts so much."

"What hurts?" Robin asked.

"Everything," Ashley said. "My body mostly."

"All right," Robin said. "You should go to a hospital. Do you have any idea where you are? Are you still in New York?"

"I don't know," Ashley wailed, and then she started sobbing.

"It's all right, Ashley," Robin said, trying to suppress all her

148

feelings of helplessness. "Do me a favor and see if there are instructions on the phone about using the 911 number in an emergency. Do you think you can do that for me?"

"Yes," Ashley sniffled. Robin waited for an endless moment, and then Ashley said, "Yeah, it says to call 911."

"Good," Robin said. "That's excellent, Ashley. All right, now, I'm going to give you some instructions, and I want you to do exactly what I tell you. All right?"

"All right," Ashley whispered, not sounding at all like herself. Robin hoped she wasn't in shock.

"After we hang up, I want you to call the 911 number," Robin said, thinking as fast as she ever had. "Now, they'll ask you where you are, and you don't know, so make sure to give them the phone number of the booth you're in. Do you see that number?"

There was another pause as Ashley searched for it. "I see it," she said.

"Good," Robin said. "I'll tell you what. You give me that number too, and that way I'll have it also."

Ashley gave her the number.

"Great," Robin declared, trying to sound cheerful. "Make sure you tell that to the 911 person. That way they can call the phone company and find out where that phone booth is located, and then they can find you."

"Boy, you're smart," Ashley said.

"Yes, I am," Robin replied. "All right, I have other things for you to do. Are you ready?"

"Umph," Ashley said.

"After you call the 911 number, I want you to stay in the phone booth," Robin said. "Just sit down and wait for them. It may take them a few minutes to find you, and if you wander off, it'll take them a lot longer. So just stay where you are, and let them rescue you."

"I don't think I can walk anymore anyway," Ashley said. "I hurt so much, Robin."

"Yeah, I know," Robin said. "Now, there's just one more thing, and then you can call the 911 number. But this is very important, and you're going to have to remember it for a while. Okay?"

"Yeah," Ashley said, her voice fading.

"When you get to the hospital, make sure to give somebody my phone number," Robin said. "Otherwise I won't know where you've been taken. If you give them my number, they'll call me and I'll be able to go to the hospital and see you right away. Can you remember that?"

"Yeah," Ashley said.

"All right," Robin said. "Tell me what you're going to do."

"Call 911," Ashley said. "Give them my phone number. Stay here. Sit down. Get rescued. Give them your number."

"Great," Robin said. "Okay, then. I'm going to hang up now, and you call 911. I'll see you just as soon as I possibly can."

"Thank you," Ashley whispered, and hung up the phone. Robin held on to hers for a moment, and then hung up also. Everything would be fine, she told herself, as long as Ashley called 911. The ambulance would find her and take her to the nearest hospital. It wasn't like Caro. Ashley would make it. She just had to. She sounded hurt, but she had managed to call Robin. It had to turn out all right.

There was no point even trying to fall back asleep, so Robin turned on a light, got dressed, and went over the conversation she'd had with Ashley a few times to see if there was anything else she should have said. Ashley was definitely coherent, which was a good sign. And she was obviously able to walk. Robin just wished she didn't know so much about internal injuries.

She sat on the bed and stared at the phone. There were people who should be told Ashley had been in an accident. The question was, when should Robin tell them? She finally decided to let Jean know immediately, mostly out of a malicious desire to wake her up. She found Jean's home number and dialed it, only to get Jean's answering machine. Jean obviously didn't have the same curfews the interns suffered from. Robin left a brief message and hung up. She then went to the bathroom and threw up, which made her feel a lot better.

Robin was reluctant to try calling Ashley back, since she didn't know what area code Ashley was in. Besides, the 911 people might want Ashley to keep the line free; it might make it easier for them to find her that way. So Robin decided to pace for a while. Then she began to pack Ashley's bags. Then she unpacked the bags, and packed an overnight bag, in case Ashley was going to be in the hospital for a day or two. She was especially proud of herself for remembering Ashley's toothbrush. She then repacked the rest of Ashley's bags, and then she paced some more.

When the phone rang, she jumped straight into the air, and then laughed at herself. The call she was expecting startled her far more than the call that woke her up. "Yes," she said into the phone, her heart pounding.

"Robin Schyler?"

"Yes," Robin said. "Speaking."

"This is Metropolitan Hospital," a woman said. "Ashley Boone gave your name as the person to be notified of her admission to the hospital."

"Yes," Robin said. "I told her to. Is she all right?"

"The doctor is examining her now," the voice said.

"Can I have your address?" Robin asked. "I'd like to come over now."

"Very well," the voice said, and gave Robin the address. Robin wrote it down and thanked the person she was talking to. They both hung up, and Robin dialed Mrs. Brundege's phone number.

"I'll meet you in the hotel lobby," Mrs. Brundege said as soon as Robin finished telling her what had happened. "I'll be over in ten minutes. Wait for me inside."

"All right," Robin said. She gathered up Ashley's overnight bag, paced awhile longer, and then went downstairs. It astounded her that Torey and Annie had slept through all that had happened.

Mrs. Brundege appeared almost immediately after Robin reached the lobby, and soon the two of them were being driven to Metropolitan Hospital. "I feel so responsible," Mrs. Brundege declared as the cab drove them to the hospital. "I pushed Ashley too hard today. We've all known Ashley had problems, and I just didn't take that into account. This is on my conscience."

"I feel responsible too," Robin said. "I should have handled her better instead of getting into a screaming fight with her."

"You've more than made up for that," Mrs. Brundege said. "You really handled things perfectly tonight, Robin. We will all be eternally grateful to you for that."

"I just hope she's okay," Robin said, holding on to Ashley's bag tightly.

The ride to the hospital seemed endless, but eventually they arrived at the emergency-room entrance. Mrs. Brundege paid for the cab, and then she and Robin walked in. Mrs. Brundege immediately took charge, and in a matter of moments she had located Ashley's doctor.

"It could have been a lot worse," the doctor told them. "Ashley's sprained her right ankle and twisted her right wrist, as well as sustaining a lot of abrasions and contusions. But she had a helmet on, so there were no head injuries, and thus far there's no sign of internal bleeding. Of course, we'll be keeping her for a couple of days just to monitor her."

Robin felt like crying from relief. Instead she said, "Could I see her now? I brought her an overnight bag."

"Are you the girl who gave her the instructions on what to do?" the doctor asked.

Robin nodded.

"Robin, right?" the doctor said. "That was impressive work. You're to be commended."

"Thank you," Robin said. "Does that mean I can see her?"

The doctor laughed. "Just for a moment," he said. "She needs her sleep. I suspect you do too." He showed Robin which way to go.

Ashley was lying on a bed, but her eyes were open. "Hi, there," Robin said. "I see you made it."

"I hurt," Ashley said.

"I bet you do," Robin said. "I brought you an overnight bag. I packed your toothbrush."

"Thank you," Ashley said. "I broke two teeth."

"Ouch," Robin said. "The doctor didn't tell us that."

"Who came with you?" Ashley asked. "Is Torey here?"

"She doesn't know yet," Robin replied. "I came with Mrs. Brundege."

"I was so rotten to Torey," Ashley said. "Does she know what I did to her?"

"She knows, and she honestly doesn't care," Robin said. "You know how Torey is. I'm sure she'll be over to visit you tomorrow. I mean today. Later."

"And you," Ashley said. "I was awful to you, wasn't I?"

"You've had better days," Robin said. "Don't worry about it, Ashley."

"I kept thinking about it while I was riding," Ashley said. "About how all I know how to do is hurt."

"Everyone makes mistakes," Robin said, wishing she could give Ashley a hug. "The trick is to learn from them."

"That's too hard," Ashley said. "I think I want to go to sleep now."

"Good idea," Robin said. "I may do that too."

"Good night," Ashley said, and moaned as she tried to adjust her body for sleep. Robin stayed for a moment, watching over her. Just as she turned to leave, she heard Ashley whisper her name.

"I'm here," Robin said softly.

"Am I ever going to see you again?" Ashley asked.

"You'll see me later today," Robin told her. "I just want to go back to our room and get some sleep."

"No," Ashley said. "I mean after I go home. You and Torey are the best friends I've ever had. Am I ever going to see you again?"

"Absolutely," Robin said, realizing with a start that she had never thought about that. "Annie too. We're a foursome, you know."

"I like having friends," Ashley whispered.

Robin stared at her for a long moment, and then heard Ashley breathing the deep regular breath of sleep. She left the room quietly and walked back to Mrs. Brundege.

"We'll go right back to the hotel," Mrs. Brundege said. "Unless you'd prefer to go back to my home. We have a guest room."

"No," Robin said. "I'll sleep better in my own room."

"Fine," Mrs. Brundege said. "How did Ashley seem to you?"

"Tired," Robin said. "And sad and in pain."

"You probably feel pretty much the same way," Mrs. Brundege said, and put her arm around Robin's shoulder. "Come on, let's get you home."

A knock on the door woke Robin late that morning. It was an effort to get out of bed, but the knocking didn't sound like it was about to go away.

"Annie made me do it," Torey said as she and Annie walked in. "She absolutely insisted we wake you up."

"That's okay," Robin said. "I should be up now anyway. What time is it?"

"Eleven," Annie said. "I just wanted you to know Mrs. Brundege called us this morning and told us what happened. We're on our way to the hospital. Do you want to come with us?"

"No," Robin said. "Later. I'll go after lunch."

"Fine," Torey said. "Now, go back to bed Robin. We'll see you later."

"No, I'm awake," Robin said. "How is Ashley, do you know?"

"Mrs. Brundege spoke to the doctor, and she said Ashley would be checked out of the hospital tomorrow," Torey replied. "I'll be flying back home with her, to make sure she gets there all right."

"You will?" Robin asked. "Whose idea was that?"

"Mine," Torey replied. "Apparently Ashley's mother didn't volunteer to come for her, and Mrs. Brundege felt somebody should go with her. She suggested Jean, and I suggested me. I won."

"I bet you did," Robin said. "Does Ashley know?"

"I'm going to tell her this morning," Torey replied. "How do you think Ashley will feel about that?"

"Very happy," Robin said. "How long will you be staying?"

"As short a time as possible," Torey said. "I want to finish my work here, after all. And there's the party in a week."

"Right," Robin said. "The party."

"We'll see you later," Annie said. "I just wanted to make sure you knew where we were and how Ashley was doing. All right?"

"Fine," Robin said, and closed the door as the girls left. Bed looked wonderful. She climbed back in, and had just fallen asleep when there was another knock to be dealt with.

Robin sighed and opened the door. Jean Kingman was standing there.

"I tried next door," Jean said, "but there was no answer. I hoped I might find all of you here."

"Annie and Torey went to the hospital," Robin told her. "Ashley was in an accident last night. Did you get my message?"

"Of course," Jean said. "I know all about the accident. That's what I wanted to talk to you about." She walked into the room, noticed the suitcases resting on Ashley's bed, and averted her eyes.

"So talk," Robin said. "I'll tell the others what you said."

"There's not much to say," Jean replied, sitting down on a chair. "It was an accident, and Ashley was very lucky to have escaped with so few injuries."

"Very lucky," Robin repeated.

"Mrs. Brundege feels terribly responsible," Jean continued. "Which is a mistake on her part, I'm sure. A lot of us had doubts about Ashley from the very beginning. She didn't make many friends for herself either, when she showed up at Mrs. Brundege's in that insane outfit, and with that very strange young man by her side. She never really seemed like a fitting representative of *Image* to me. She had too much flair. Girls with that much flair almost always end up in trouble."

"If you say so," Robin said, yawning.

"But the fashion department does like flair," Jean said, shrugging her shoulders. "They don't worry about the consequences." She pursed her lips. "In any event, I trust I can count on you and the others not to go around telling people just what happened last night."

"I don't know," Robin said. "It depends who you mean by 'people.' "

"The press comes to mind," Jean said. "Of course, what happened was an accident, but nonetheless, there are papers in this city that would publish a story like this. '*Image* intern gets kicked off the staff for theft, borrows her punk-rock boyfriend's motorcycle, and ends up crashing into a telephone pole in the middle of nowhere.' There are a lot of papers that could turn that story into a juicy scandal."

"We won't tell the press," Robin promised. "Or radio or TV."

"Good," Jean said. "I was sure I could count on you for that. As far as the people at *Image* go, the ones who have to know have been informed already. The rest can make up whatever story they want. The truth will come out eventually, but by then Ashley will be safely back home."

Robin thought about Ashley safely back home, and the lengths she was willing to go to avoid returning there.

"Of course you can tell your families," Jean persisted. "But that can wait until you're home too. Why worry your parents unduly? Let them see for themselves what a fabulous summer you all have had, and then tell them about Ashley's little accident."

"Please leave now, Jean," Robin said. "I'm not in the mood to listen to any more of this."

"Certainly," Jean said, rising from the chair. "By the way, Robin, we were all very impressed with how you handled yourself in this crisis. You scored a lot of points for yourself. I don't know how Mrs. Brundege plans on expressing her gratitude and appreciation, but I'm sure she'll think of something appropriate."

"Great," Robin said. "Good-bye, Jean."

"Good-bye, Robin," Jean said. "I'm sure you'll feel better after you get a little more sleep." She smiled at Robin and left the room.

Robin curled back up in bed, but she knew she wouldn't be able to fall back asleep. Her mind was racing far too fast, thinking about Ashley and the summer and accidents. And suddenly all she could think about was Caro, and there was no point trying to stop the memories from filling her. She didn't cry, though, which surprised her. She just remembered the pain and the sorrow and the aching sense of loss.

But then she started remembering the good times. Those were the tricky memories, the ones she usually tried to suppress. Because when she remembered how much she'd loved Caro, and Caro's pleasure in life, the pain always grew sharper, more cutting. It was easier to remember Caro in her hospital bed than to remember Caro raking the leaves or playing badminton or doing cartwheels in the living room. But today when Caro smiled, Robin smiled with her. When Caro laughed, Robin laughed with her. And while knowing that Caro was gone still hurt, it didn't lessen the pleasure of the memories.

Caro was dead, but she had lived, and that was the important thing. She had given Robin so much that Robin hadn't had the chance to appreciate. She'd given her the strength to face another person's pain, and courage to search for the right answers. Without that, Robin didn't know if she could have helped Ashley last night. She might have hung up in anger just at the sound of Ashley's voice. Or, more likely, she might have panicked, not known what to say, and left Ashley alone, unable to help herself. And then anything could have happened to her. But Robin hadn't made those mistakes. She had finally been able to help.

There was nothing she could have done for Caro, she knew. No magic incantations that could have saved her life. And there would probably be a million situations in the future when she would be just as helpless, just as out of control. But she could always know that at least once, she had made a difference. And that was an extraordinarily special feeling.

She opened her eyes and stared at Ashley's sad little travel clock. It was close to one, and she was still in bed. So she finally got up, took a shower, and dressed. She'd be going to the hospital later, but first she wanted to see Tim and tell him what had happened. When he answered the phone, she gave him a short version of what had happened since last night.

"I'll be right over," he said. "I'll meet you downstairs."

Robin hung up the phone and realized she no longer wanted

157

to be in her hotel room. She'd rather wait in the lobby, she decided, so she locked the door and took the elevator down. It felt good to be in a public place. As she found a seat in the lobby, she saw Annie enter.

"I'm waiting for Tim," Robin told her.

"Good," Annie said. "I'll keep you company until he shows."

"I'd like that," Robin said.

"You know, I haven't had a chance to tell you how much I admire what you did last night," Annie said. "The way you handled Ashley's phone call."

"I did what I had to," Robin said, but then she smiled. "I do feel good about it, though."

"You ought to," Annie replied. "I left Torey at the hospital so she and Ashley could talk for a while in private. I could see Ashley wanted that."

"I'm sure she did," Robin said. "It was good of you to notice."

They sat there silently. "I think you're pretty terrific," Annie finally declared. "You're just about as good as your mother is always telling my mother."

Robin laughed. "You hold up your end pretty well also," she said.

"I'm glad we're cousins," Annie said. "I'm sorry we lost each other, and I'm glad we had a chance to find each other again. I don't want to lose this feeling."

"We won't," Robin promised. "There's been too much loss already. I'm not taking any more."

"Good," Annie said, and gave Robin a hug. "Oh, there's Tim. I'll give you a chance to be alone with him now."

"Thanks, Annie," Robin said. Annie got up and walked over to the elevator. Robin walked to the door by herself and joined Tim there.

They embraced for a moment and then kissed. "I love you," Tim said. "I love you and I don't want to lose you, and it's already Saturday and we have so little time."

"We have what we need," Robin told him. "Come on. Let's turn a week into forever."